Son [illegible]

THE DEVIL AND THE DANCER

Chloe Reardon has a problem, and his name is Gavin Wallace.

Okay, Gavin isn't exactly a problem unless you consider a highly attractive wind vampire with dubious intentions a problem. Especially if that vampire is your boss and has an affinity for kilts and excellent taste in music.

None of that matters though, because Chloe Reardon has had enough of dangerous men. Danger is overrated. Danger is the opposite of sexy. So Gavin is the last man—or vampire—on earth she needs to let into her heart.

But what if the most dangerous man you know is also the one who makes you feel the strongest?

The Devil and the Dancer is a paranormal romance novella in the Elemental Legacy series.

PRAISE FOR ELIZABETH HUNTER

Elizabeth Hunter's books are delicious and addicting, like the best kind of chocolate. She hooked me from the first page, and her stories just keep getting better and better. Paranormal romance fans won't want to miss this exciting author!

— Thea Harrison, NYT bestselling author

Developing compelling and unforgettable characters is a real Hunter strength as she proves yet again with Kyra and Leo. Another amazing novel by a master storyteller!

— RT Magazine

This book more than lived up to the expectations I had, in fact it blew them out of the water.

— This Literary Life

A towering work of romantic fantasy that will captivate the reader's mind and delight their heart. Elizabeth Hunter's ability to construct such a sumptuous narrative time and time again is nothing short of amazing.

— The Reader Eater

For David
My rock
I am so blessed to call you mine.

The Devil and the Dancer

ISBN: 9781798422519

Cover: Damonza
Content Editor: Amy Cissell, Cissell Ink
Copy Editor: Anne Victory
Proofreader: Linda, Victory Editing

Recurve Press LLC
PO Box 4034
Visalia, California
USA
ElizabethHunterWrites.com

THE DEVIL AND THE DANCER

AN ELEMENTAL LEGACY NOVELLA

ELIZABETH HUNTER

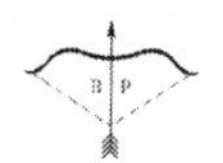

1

The letter was like a dozen others on the surface. It committed to nothing. It was a test.

Of what, Gavin Wallace wasn't certain.

The writer of the letter corresponded with him regularly. They weren't friends. They never would be. But their connection couldn't be denied. It definitely could not be ignored.

I am thinking about coming to New York City. Your introduction to the O'Brien would be most welcome. This is regarding a business matter, not a personal one.

Vivian

Gavin didn't need to breathe. No physical compulsion demanded it. He was a wind vampire who didn't need to inhale or exhale except to smell the air and to speak. He could hold his breath for as long as necessary and not feel the effects.

So the sigh that left his lungs was entirely one of habit.

Vivian.

Was it truly a business matter, or did she have an ulterior motive? It would be impossible to tell until he talked to her, but he suspected the latter; Vivian always had an ulterior motive.

A laugh made him look up and across the bar. The smile that touched his lips was as much a habit as the sigh that had come before. The smile, however, was far more recent.

Watching Chloe Reardon talk to the bar patrons was one of his favorite pastimes. He pretended to do paperwork, sort through letters, or read a magazine while he surreptitiously observed her chatting with a regular, polishing glasses, or advising one of the younger servers.

She was a woman who could enjoy talking to anyone. It was a skill Gavin had never developed, even with over a century of life behind him. If he had his way, he'd be more likely to sit in a corner and look aloof.

It wasn't the most advantageous attitude for a publican. And even after many years, dozens of properties, and millions in hidden accounts, that was still what Gavin considered himself. He was a barman, and he was a good one. Of course, part of the reason he was good was that he excelled at the one skill every publican needed.

Gavin Wallace was a genius at reading people. He understood what they wanted, and he knew what to give them to get what he desired.

Sometimes all a human or an immortal needed was the right drink and the right ear. Blood or wine or whiskey. Gavin didn't need to be Captain Sunshine to supply those.

Other times it was an introduction or an invitation. For vampires, it was often a safe place to meet a dangerous person.

Gavin provided any or all those things, and in exchange he received wealth, safety, and influence, which he wielded very, very judiciously.

"Boss, you want another?" A server was standing at the edge of the table with a golden glass of whiskey on a tray.

Gavin glanced up. "Thank you, Priscilla."

"No problem." She set down the drink. "Let me know if you want something to eat. Raf is just about to shut down the kitchen."

"Sounds good." Gavin looked over to the bar as he raised his glass and sipped the unlabeled scotch he kept in a small cupboard. It was from his own distillery, but it wasn't in his nature to advertise he owned it.

Chloe caught his gaze and offered him a quick smile before she returned her attention to the human across the counter.

And what do you need, Chloe Reardon?

Space.

And time.

Damn my luck.

She laughed at something the customer said. It was an older man, a stage manager for one of the larger off-Broadway theaters if Gavin's memory served him correctly. Gavin didn't know how the man knew Chloe, but familiarity radiated between the two. She reached for the bottle of Jim Beam without the customer asking, filled his glass before she read another order and shook two gin cocktails, all the while nodding while the older man told a story.

She'd been working for Gavin over a year. She was a gold-star employee, the kind immortals valued above the common swarm of humanity. She was trustworthy and discreet. She was independent and considerate. Smart, quick, and flexible. Aware of vampires without being fearful of them.

Chloe was also a brilliant and bright young woman. A gifted artist and a good friend. She was wise and funny, empathetic and loyal.

Chloe Reardon was everything that made Gavin feel like living again, but for the first time in 120 years, he found something he couldn't win in trade.

He couldn't buy her.

He couldn't barter for her.

He wanted to seduce her—fucking hell, he wanted to seduce her.

But more, he wanted her to be *his*. Of her own choice. He wanted her to come to him, surrender, throw her lot into the darkness with him.

In the year since they'd met, her surrender had become his singular desire.

But it had to be her own.

So he became the patient suitor. He took her to shows and dinners and parties. He gave her a safe room in his home. Ever the gentleman, he demanded nothing but made it clear she could take anything she wanted.

Gavin was starting to believe they would never move past the strange neutral zone they existed in. The thought made him edgy. He was a patient predator, but he needed an end in sight. He needed to make her… just a little uncomfortable.

It was a risk, but one he felt he had to take. After all, Gavin Wallace was a genius at knowing what people needed. And though he knew Chloe needed time and space, he fervently believed she also needed something else.

She needed him.

She felt Gavin's eyes on her back as they walked from the pub to the corner where he had a car waiting, and Chloe would be lying if the idea didn't put just a little more sway in her hips. In the year since they'd met, the idea of his eyes on her had become welcome. Enticing instead of intimidating.

"Your rehearsal is at what time tomorrow?" Gavin's right hand came to the small of her back. His left reached for the messenger bag she carried, which he slipped off her shoulder and slung over his.

"Eleven. I can carry that, you know."

"But why not let me?" He brushed a kiss across her temple as he walked beside her. "Good. You can get six hours in tonight and take a nap in the afternoon."

"Is Veronica working tomorrow?"

"I believe so, but you know she won't bother you unless you need something."

Veronica was Gavin's house manager, his day person, and an utter and complete professional. Chloe found her competence a tad intimidating even if Veronica was polite at all times.

All of Gavin's people were professionals, from Veronica to the security crew she'd met, his business manager to his sommelier. They were all professionals. Gavin surrounded himself with professionals.

If it weren't for her, Ben, and Tenzin, Chloe wondered if he'd interact with anyone he didn't employ.

"Did you see the invitation from Cormac?" Chloe asked.

"I did."

She watched him from the corner of her eye. "Did anything seem strange about it to you?"

The corner of his mouth turned up. "No."

"It was addressed to both of us."

His fingers curled into her back. "Because I believe he wants both of us to attend the reception."

"It was addressed to both of us at your address."

He paused and nudged her to stand in front of him, pressing her closer. "Is that a problem?"

"I don't know." Was it? It seemed like everyone knew she stayed with Gavin regularly, and as far as Chloe knew, she was his only regular social companion. She was his plus-one. And if she couldn't attend something with him, he went alone. "It's fine," she whispered.

He angled his head and bent down. "Good." His lips moved softly over the arch of her cheek. "You smell lovely tonight."

"I spilled Knob Creek on my shirt."

"Aye, I know." His mouth moved to the side, and she felt his breath tickle the sensitive skin under her ear. "I don't mind a little Southern flavor, Miss Reardon."

Chloe had learned that Gavin's Scottish came out when he was angry—which happened rarely—or turned on, which happened regularly. Much of the time, Americans mistook him for English.

He wasn't. He'd made that very clear.

"Shall I see if you've spilled any other spirits?" His mouth moved to the other side of her neck. "Do I detect a bit of Cointreau here?" His tongue licked her skin, and she gripped his shoulders. "Sweet."

She was going to melt into a puddle. "The car is waiting."

"Aye, I pay it to do that."

Her head spun at the low timbre of his voice.

"*One day soon, Chloe Reardon.*" The memory of his furious kiss a year ago hadn't become any less potent with time.

Gavin took one more long breath at her neck before he pulled away, put his arm around her, and kept walking. "The reception on Friday sounds like a waste of time. If you don't want to go, I'll make our excuses to Cormac."

"It's fine." She cleared her throat and tried to focus on walking toward the waiting car without her knees buckling. "The artist sounds interesting."

"If you want to go, we'll go. You won't be the only human there." He opened the door and ushered her inside.

"Oh. That'll be nice." She settled in and buckled her seat belt just as the driver pulled into the sparse middle-of-the-night traffic. Chloe felt the day catch up with her as she leaned into the plush sedan seat and closed her eyes. Gavin shifted beside her, his electric presence filling her senses even as she drifted with exhaustion.

When she'd first left her abusive ex and moved in with her

friend Ben and his vampire partner, Tenzin, she'd had no idea that vampires existed. She'd always known Ben's family was a little strange, but in the past year she'd become ever more immersed in the immortal world. She knew Ben had mixed feelings about it, but Chloe had walked in with her eyes open.

After all, while vampires could be horrible, so could human beings. She knew that firsthand. On balance, she'd had more compassion and patience from the vampires in her life than most of the humans. Ben's aunt and uncle made her feel like part of their family. Tenzin was one of the oddest friends she'd ever made. She was also one of the most loyal.

And Gavin?

She didn't know what she was to Gavin, but it was something. She knew he wanted to sleep with her and that he was protective. Past that? She had no idea.

She'd worked for him over a year, following him from his first New York pub, the Bat and Barrel, to his newest venture in Hell's Kitchen, the Dancing Bear. It was an easy job made easier by the fact that everyone at the bar assumed she was in a relationship with the boss, so no one messed with her.

Which she was. They had a relationship. She wasn't sure exactly what that relationship was, but it was a relationship.

Chloe didn't care that everyone assumed she was sleeping with Gavin. They had every reason to assume it even though she had her own room at his house. She stayed at his place on nights when she had early rehearsal the next day or just needed a break from the blistering chemistry growing between Ben and Tenzin at their loft.

Gavin was a picture of patience, but he had his limits. She didn't push him and he didn't push her.

Someone needs to push someone soon, her libido shouted. *This is getting ridiculous.*

Ridiculous maybe. But also safe.

Chloe liked safety. She liked knowing what to expect. She'd spent years with Tom never knowing when the next blow would come or what would precipitate the next argument. She'd fallen in love with Tom partly because he was "edgy," which to an overprotected girl from Southern California felt exciting and forbidden.

She'd learned her lesson. Edgy wasn't exciting. Edgy was painful. Edgy was dangerous. Edgy could get your bones broken, your body bruised, and your dreams crushed.

What boggled her mind—what she still couldn't make sense of—was why Gavin, who was exponentially more dangerous than her human ex could ever dream of being, had become her anchor of safety in the strange new immortal world she'd entered.

She knew Gavin wasn't safe, and there was no way he wasn't dangerous.

"A good man would stop pursuing you. A deserving one would wait. He'd be patient. I'm not a good man."

His words said one thing. His actions another.

Which was she supposed to believe when her heart was pulling her in one direction and her head was pulling in the other?

She was nearly sleeping when they reached his apartment. Gavin was tempted to lift her in his arms, but he knew she didn't like it. She didn't like being carted around unless it was with a dance partner.

You should learn to dance with her.

He should do lots of things. He should be more empathetic to homeless people. He should donate more to the environment. And he should take the dance classes Chloe teased him about. But what vampire took ballroom dance classes? Gavin wasn't the dancing type, even if he had a keen appreciation for the art form. He always went to Chloe's shows, and he'd bought season tickets to the ballet. He even watched the horrid dancing reality show she was addicted to on the television. Mostly he appreciated watching Chloe dance around the room he'd had retrofitted for her.

"Wow! I can't believe your apartment came with a studio like this."

"I know. I was shocked myself. Not sure what I'll do with the space, but you're welcome to use it while you're here."

He'd had the gym renovated with mirrors, a wooden floor, and a practice barre two months after they'd met. It had taken less than a week when the right money was thrown at the project.

It had been an impulse decision. Gavin didn't usually get impulsive about humans. So when he felt the urge, he indulged it. Luckily, it had garnered many hours of pleasure for both Chloe and himself. Chloe because she liked to dance. Gavin because he liked to watch her.

He leaned across the back seat and touched her cheek. "Home, dove."

She sighed and leaned toward him. "Huh?"

"We're home." He ran a finger down her cheek and slung her messenger bag over his shoulder. "Fucking hell, woman, what do you keep in this thing?"

Her eyes were still closed. "Contact lens stuff. Glasses. Change of clothes. Leggings. Shoes."

"When are you going to start leaving things here? Your room has a closet bigger than most East Village apartments."

Her eyes flickered open. "Pushy."

Gavin shook his head and opened his car door, waiting outside for her to wake up and join him. The driver sat idling and silent while Gavin stood, his jaw clenched.

Pushy? For fuck's sake, he was anything *but* pushy. If he was pushy, she'd have been in his bed months ago. If he was pushy, Chloe Reardon would be in his thrall.

You don't want that.

Chloe got out of the car and walked around to him, rubbing her eyes. "I'm sorry."

"It's fine."

"You say that"—she stood in front of him as the car pulled away—"but your tone says you're pissed off at me."

Gavin walked toward the elevator. "You're tired. I don't want to talk about this right now."

Chloe followed him. "I shouldn't have called you pushy. You're not pushy. You're like... the opposite of pushy."

He pressed the button to call the elevator and felt the air stir across his skin. He needed a nice long flight tonight. Needed the wind across his skin. Needed—

Chloe nudged his arm out of the way, slid her hand across his back and into the rear pocket of his trousers.

Gavin looked down in surprise. "Miss Reardon, you have your hand on my arse."

The corner of her mouth quirked up. "Are you complaining?"

"I don't know," he muttered. "You're being a bit pushy."

Her laugh was punctuated by a small snort, and Gavin broke into a smile. She started to slide her hand out of his pocket, but he grabbed it and kept it exactly where she'd put it.

"Are you planning to keep that there all the way up to the penthouse?"

"Are you worried someone has seen you stake your claim? It's three in the morning; I think we have the elevator to ourselves."

Her cheeks flushed a little. "Stake my claim?"

"It's about fucking time, I'll add. I like it when you get territorial."

She pressed her face into his shoulder. "I'm never going to hear the end of this."

"No." He chuckled. "If I could get the angle right, I'd take a picture."

He watched her laughing against his shoulder, ridiculously pleased that she was sleepy and silly and walking home with him. That she trusted him. That she looked at him and didn't see a monster but a man.

Oh, fuck me. Gavin felt his heart thump twice.

He didn't just want Chloe Reardon. He was in love with her.

2

Chloe watched Ben stride through the loft, tossing phone chargers and batteries next to his backpack on the couch.

"We'll be in pretty remote areas at times, so use the satellite phone if my mobile doesn't work."

"Uh-huh."

"From what I've heard, nothing is reliable. Not power. Not cell signal. I'm bringing the solar chargers, so we should be fine with the satellite phone."

"But only for emergencies," Chloe said. "Tell Tenzin I'm not calling her to report on the flowers blooming."

"I'll let her know, but..."

"No! Enough. She's obsessing." It was true. Tenzin didn't do slight interest. If something caught her attention, that interest quickly turned into obsession. In the year Chloe had been living at the apartment, she'd seen it happen half a dozen times.

"That's what she does." Ben shrugged. "And you have to admit the garden does look really good."

Ben had relented and allowed Tenzin to plant a full garden on the roof, including fruit trees, a water feature, and a fire pit.

"Just tell her she has to trust that I will not kill all her plants. She's showed me what to do at least a dozen times. And you guys are going to Puerto Rico, not Kathmandu."

Ben squinted. "Do you know where Kathmandu is?"

"Do you?"

"Nepal."

Chloe threw a balled-up sock at him. "Fine, know-it-all. Still, it's like four hours from New York, not the ends of the earth. I'll survive without you two."

"If you need money—"

"I have access to Tenzin's account here."

Tenzin's mind-boggling account.

Chloe had no idea how much money Tenzin actually had, but the account Chloe used to pay bills and run Tenzin's financial life was... intimidating. Chloe could buy a modestly priced home in Queens with the cash Tenzin kept available.

But most of the time Chloe tried not to think about how much Ben and Tenzin spent on anything. She knew how much the remodel was—roughly—but Ben had instructed the builders to send all bills to him. Everything in New York City cost a fortune, even for someone accustomed to Los Angeles. So she gritted her teeth, let Ben pay for everything, and plotted how long it would take for her to get her own place.

Not that she didn't like living in the loft. She was ridiculously grateful, enjoyed working for Tenzin, and often felt like she had the entire place to herself. Tenzin had been unusually quiet the past six months, Ben was gone a lot, and Chloe was often the only one awake during daylight hours.

She was slowly making new friends. She and Arthur had grown close again, though the hilarious designer was somewhat obsessed with her employers. Gavin spent a lot of time with her, but he was more comfortable in the bar or at his place.

He'd once muttered something about "territories being a bit complicated."

I like it when you get territorial.

The memory brought a flush to her cheeks. Chloe had no idea what Gavin meant by territories. She had no idea how a lot of stuff in the vampire world worked. She didn't want to know too much. She had her people—and her vampires—but she did not want to get deeper into the sticky politics of immortal life.

Ben and Tenzin would be in Puerto Rico looking for pirate treasure for about a month. While they were gone, Chloe wouldn't have much to do other than watch the house, pay the bills, and do any research online that Tenzin wasn't able to do herself. Half the time that research would involve whatever mysterious artifact or treasure they were following.

The other half would be how to make a cake in a microwave or why Americans called the back of a car the trunk instead of the boot.

This was her life.

A few more minutes with Ben didn't reassure Chloe that he was headed anywhere productive for himself personally, despite the fact that her friend had actual human relatives on the island.

She walked downstairs to the training area to find Tenzin, her employer and her oddest friend, staring at a group of weapons spread across the training area.

"What are you doing?" Chloe asked.

"Trying to decide what to take."

Chloe blinked. "You're bringing a sword to Puerto Rico? Why?"

"I always carry at least one sword with me at all times. Usually two." She looked up. "Arthur made me a new coat."

"I don't want to know." Arthur probably knew deep down there was something wrong with Tenzin. He just found the ancient vampire too hilarious to examine the instinct closely. "Is that... allowed?"

Tenzin turned to Chloe with a frown. "Is what allowed?"

"Can you just bring a sword into a foreign country? Is that allowed?"

Tenzin narrowed her eyes. "Who exactly do you think would be inspecting *me*?"

"Okay. I hadn't thought about that." Because *of course* no one was inspecting Tenzin. If Gavin flew to Puerto Rico, no one would inspect him either. It wasn't as if there was a wind vampire hanging around in Puerto Rican airspace to TSA the vampires coming onto the island.

"Right." She looked at the collection of swords Tenzin had pulled onto the ground. "I'm going to say the one with the curved blade and the brown leather handle—"

"The Ottoman pala saber. Good choice."

"—because it's relatively short and looks kinda like a

pirate sword, which is cool. And then... the triangular grip sword thingy with the jeweled handle."

"It's an Indian punch dagger or a katar. Excellent choice."

"It looks very lethal and is probably pretty easy to hide except for all those crystals on the handle."

"Those are emeralds."

Of course they are! Chloe shook her head. "Okay. So I guess those two."

Tenzin patted her shoulder. "You give excellent advice."

"I try." She turned to the small vampire, who was already putting away the dozen swords she wasn't taking to Puerto Rico in her new jacket. "I need you to promise me something."

Tenzin froze. She turned slowly. "I do not make promises lightly."

"I know you don't."

Humor had fled Tenzin's expression. "What is it?"

"I know neither of us can make Ben do anything he doesn't want to do. He acts all easygoing, but he's like a mule sometimes."

"I've mentally compared him to a donkey many times in my head."

"Yeah, so..." Chloe took a breath. "You know he has family there."

"Yes."

"I think he really needs to see them. Not for them. For himself. For his own sanity. I know it's been bothering him." She cleared her throat. "We both have a lot of issues with our families. But for him..."

"He made very adult decisions when he was only a boy."

Chloe nodded. "At least I was eighteen. I had a little more perspective. But I think he was ten the last time he saw his grandmother."

Tenzin nodded.

"Just try. Do your best. I don't want to interfere with your job down there, but I just think... it'd be really good for him."

Tenzin looked at Chloe for a long time before she spoke. "I will do what I can. I promise."

"Thank you."

"And I want you to do something for me in return."

Chloe nodded. "No problem. What—?"

"You and Gavin should have sex. The tension is really becoming bothersome, and I can tell both of you want to. Do it while Ben is gone, that way there won't be a strange reaction from him because you're his childhood girlfriend and Gavin is his friend."

Chloe let out a slow breath. "That was *so* not what I was expecting you to ask me."

"Also, I want to start gathering my own mushrooms, because the farmers who sell them at the market are thieves. Can you find some kind of guide for that?"

Bizarre pronouncement and obscure task. That was much more like Tenzin.

Chloe nodded. "I'll see what I can do."

Chloe closed her eyes and leaned into Gavin's shoulder,

letting the hot bubbling water soothe the muscles she'd worked that evening during rehearsal. "I'm worried about him."

"He'll be fine." Gavin rubbed her shoulders. "He's traveled in far more dangerous places than Puerto Rico. From what I've heard, most of the power has been restored—even in more remote parts—and the infrastructure is clawing back. Ben has excellent survival skills. Puerto Rico will not be a challenge."

"I'm not worried about him surviving. Tenzin will be with him once he gets to San Juan. Tenzin won't let anything happen to Ben. That's not what I'm worried about."

"Then what?"

Chloe struggled with how much to share with Gavin. "I'm worried about him... personally."

"Personally?" Gavin tilted her chin to the side so he could look at her face. "Does he have family there?"

Chloe sighed. "I can't say."

"I know he's part Puerto Rican. He's mentioned as much in passing. It didn't even occur to me that he might have living family." Gavin frowned. "I assumed Giovanni had adopted an orphan."

"I don't want to break confidence. Just know that most of Ben's childhood was awful."

"That much is evident." He stroked curly wisps of hair back from her forehead and kissed her temple. "There's a look a person comes to recognize after a hundred years or so. One can tell which humans have lived hard lives and which have not. Some vampires take advantage of that." His hand stopped moving. "I've taken advantage of that, I'm sorry to say. Or at least I did in the past."

"And now?"

He wrapped his arm around her waist. "It would make me a sad kind of thing to prey on the wounded, don't you think? That's what I realized. Humans only have a few years at the end of the day. It's not for me to make their lives more difficult when their own kind do that enough."

The sharp twist in her chest was familiar now, though no less painful.

"Only a few years."

He was right. Compared to Gavin, Chloe only had a handful of years. She would be a few fleeting moments in his very long life. Despite what Tenzin had encouraged her to do, despite what she wanted for herself, nothing about being with Gavin was simple.

You and Gavin should have sex. The tension is really becoming bothersome, and I can tell both of you want to.

If only it was a matter of what she wanted.

"Anyway..." Gavin poured warm water over shoulders that had gone cold. "Ben has that look. I always assumed he'd had a hard childhood. He used to be much easier to read, you know. He's a bit foggy now."

"Foggy?"

"Give him a few years and he'll be as hard to read as his uncle. Of course, he'll likely be a vampire by then. Are you ready for that?"

Chloe's eyes went wide and she spun around. Her head was full, examining the layers of everything sex with Gavin would entail. What did he mean? *Was she ready for that?* Did he expect her to become a vampire? Did he *want* her to? Did that mean he wanted them to be more? What did *more* even mean?

"Ready for *what*?" she asked.

Gavin frowned. "For Ben to be a vampire."

Her heart slowed down. "Oh. That."

His eyebrows went up. "Did you think—?"

"No, of course not."

"Because that's... that's a conversation."

God, let me die now. Twenty-five years has been long enough. This wouldn't be a bad time to go. "I didn't. I mean, I don't... That's not something we need to talk about."

Yes, please. Just let me die.

"Ever?" Gavin stared at her, that deep, penetrating stare that asked Chloe for everything and offered more than she was ready to receive.

"Don't ask me yet," she whispered. *Okay God. Never mind. I could use a few more years.*

Gavin touched her chin with the tip of his finger, drew it up and around her lips, tracing the sensitive outline before he leaned in and took her mouth. His kiss spun her around and unraveled her. Every time. She could feel the iron control in his shoulders when she placed her hands there. Feel the desire he leashed for her.

The quick inhale at her neck. The tightening fist in her hair. He pulled her to straddle his waist, holding her thigh just above the knee. His hand, like the rest of him, was just as controlled. Firm grip on heated flesh.

Chloe was the soft to his hard, melting into his chest and letting her muscles rest against his. Her breasts to his chest. Her mouth soft and yielding to his.

He pulled away. "Chloe, ye make ma heid mince."

She leaned forward and pressed her face into his neck, putting her lips against the place where his heart should beat. It only gave the occasional flutter, usually when he was aroused.

Why do you still wait, Gavin Wallace? Haven't you gotten tired of me yet?

She didn't say those things—didn't even want to think them—but they were the voice in her head. The constant, nagging whisper that tried to convince her she shouldn't get too attached, shouldn't let her guard down too much.

He ran his fingers up and down her spine, massaging the bare edge of her glute with such perfect pressure she wanted him to go farther down. Under the bathing suit. Bare skin to bare skin.

And then what?

Chloe took a deep breath and lay against his chest, allowing herself the pleasure of his touch for as long as he was willing to offer it.

Gavin was a dazzling predator, a powerful and rich immortal with connections she knew nothing about and influence she didn't stop to ponder. He didn't flaunt any of it. He wore power like one of his perfectly tailored suits.

He'll get bored with you eventually. Probably right after you agree to have sex with him.

He didn't push, and she hesitated. They were in stalemate, a pair of would-be lovers, both too cautious to make the first move after months and months of foreplay. She didn't know what kind of status she had in Gavin's world other than she was under Ben's uncle's aegis and vampires at the bar no longer flirted with her.

At all.

She knew they considered her Gavin's... something. She had no idea what that something was. No doubt they assumed she was his lover. That they slept together. That he fed from her.

A frisson over her skin.

Gavin's hands stopped and pressed in. "What are you thinking about right now?"

Remember, Chloe. He knows when you're turned on.

Sometimes living around vampires made Chloe seriously want to die. They smelled everything. They heard everything. The silent burp you managed to hide on your date? Not hidden if that date was a vampire. No bodily function was a mystery to them.

"What were ye thinkin' about?" he whispered.

The mental image leaped to the front of her mind. Gavin's fangs, long in his mouth, breaking her skin.

Her body responded.

His hands gripped tighter. "Chloe?"

"What do you think I was thinking about?"

"Sex."

She laughed. "I wasn't actually. But that's a good guess."

"So not sex. Now I'm even more curious." His fingers went to work again, stroking up and down her back, teasing the top of her ass, the small of her back, the curve of her neck—

"Hmmm." He trailed a hand down her arm. "Goose bumps again."

The hand went back to her neck. His lips followed. Gavin held the hair at her nape and tugged, pulling her head back and exposing her throat to the cold night air and his mouth.

Goose bumps. She felt them everywhere.

Gavin kissed across her collarbone. "Were ye thinking about me biting ye?"

Her heart took off at a gallop just as his lips reached her pulse point.

"I think ye were," he murmured. "And I think ye fancy the idea."

God yes, I love the idea, and I must be going crazy.

Chloe shut her eyes and said nothing.

"Just so ye know," Gavin said. "When I bite you, I *will* enjoy a taste from yer pretty neck." He nipped her skin lightly. "But when I'm really hungry"—his hand slipped from the top of her thigh to the inside, dragging up, up, up until Chloe gasped—"there's nothing like a nice bite right here." He pinched the soft flesh just below the juncture of her thighs. "When I'm *really* hungry."

Without another word, Gavin slid her to the side, leaving her breathless on the bench of the hot tub as he stood and climbed out, sporting an erection that made Chloe think very unprofessional thoughts about her employer.

She wasn't going to whimper. She refused.

But she wasn't going to sleep much either.

GAVIN TOOK a deep breath when he reached the solarium that led to the stairs of his penthouse. Leaving Chloe in the hot tub, wet and ready for him, was one of the hardest things—no pun intended—he'd done in over a hundred years.

"You're playing the long game," he muttered. "It's worth it."

He'd been wooing the woman for months, seducing her in slow bites and always leaving her hungry for more. Tonight, when she'd inadvertently brought up turning and then—*fuck* his luck—Gavin feeding from her, he'd nearly lost his mind. Between that and the realization he'd had the night before, his lust *and* his bloodlust were raging.

He gripped the erection that threatened to rip his swimming suit and tried to think about anything but Chloe. Outside. On his roof. Hot and wet and—

"I'm a fucking numpty. Why did I leave?" He was just about to walk back outside when the house phone rang.

Walking over to the small desk, he punched the speakerphone button. "Whoever this is, you'd better have an excellent reason for calling."

3

He listened to the voice on the other end of the line without flinching.

"Tell me why," he demanded.

"I told you, it's a business matter."

"It's never only a business matter, Vivian. Not with you."

Her laugh grated against his skin and killed any hint of arousal Chloe had provoked.

"Don't you trust me?" she asked.

"Not even a little."

"I'll be there in a few days," she said. "I didn't hear back from you, so this is your courtesy call. I'll expect an introduction, *mon loup*."

He squeezed his eyes shut. "Who are you bringing with you?"

"Renard, of course."

"He has Veronica's information. Tell him to call her with details."

"Very well. I'm dying to see your new place, Gavin. I hear it's quite delicious."

Even the way she said his name grated. *Gahveen.*

"I'll see you next week." He hung up the phone. She didn't afford him any courtesy, so why should he give her any? She would intrude in his life at her leisure with no consideration for him. Vivian didn't ask permission. She assumed.

Gavin wrapped a thick towel around himself and grabbed another for Chloe. She'd said she wanted to spend the night at the loft since Ben and Tenzin were leaving for Puerto Rico soon. It was time for her to go.

He hit another button on the phone. "Abraham."

"Yes, boss?"

"Chloe needs a ride back to the loft. Fifteen minutes, please."

"Of course."

Vivian and Chloe. A knot of dread settled in Gavin's stomach. He didn't want Vivian to know anything about Chloe. Not yet. She'd know eventually if things went according to his plans, but the longer he could put it off, the easier life would be.

He walked back outside and saw her with her eyes closed, leaning against the side of the hot tub. Beads of sweat ran down her temples, following the line of her graceful neck.

Vivian wouldn't touch her. She was too precious. Too breakable.

"Chloe." He spoke from a distance.

She opened her eyes. "Hey." Her voice was a little breathless. Unlike Gavin, who'd had cold water doused on him by Vivian's phone call, Chloe was still breathless and wanting.

Fuck me.

"I'm very sorry"—he had to make his voice brusque —"but I'm going to have to leave. I thought I had more time tonight, but I don't."

She frowned and sat up straight. "Oh. Um... okay. Should I call Abe—?"

"I already called him. He'll be waiting downstairs in fifteen minutes." He carefully placed the towel next to the hot tub on the redwood bench and stepped back. "If you don't need me—"

"I'm fine." Her eyes revealed her confusion. "Go... do what you need to do. Everything all right at the bar?"

"Yes." He wanted to reassure her somehow, but he didn't want to explain Vivian. "There's something I have to talk to Cormac about. It came up at the last minute."

"Right." Chloe climbed out of the hot tub, steam rising from her glowing brown skin.

Gavin wanted to bite her. He wanted to wrap her up in the soft towel and cart her to his bed. He couldn't do any of those things. Not with Vivian's arrival hanging over his head.

Chloe wrapped the towel around herself and forced a smile to her lips. "Okay. See you."

He bent down and kissed the arch of her cheek. "Tomorrow night. Sleep well, dove."

The endearment softened her expression, but only a little. "Night. I'll see you after rehearsal tomorrow. I'm working until closing."

"Good."

Gavin walked back in the house and down to his office before he could do or say anything that would reveal the churning anger in his belly. He wasn't angry with Chloe, and he didn't want her to even entertain the thought. The inevitable mess that Vivian would bring was not her concern. He only hoped he could shield her from it for a little while longer.

"I DON'T KNOW." Chloe sat on the ground, stretching her hamstrings while Arthur took measurements from her partner. "He was... distant. Not like himself. It was weird."

"Chloe, all your friends are weird," the costume designer mumbled through lips holding pins.

"Except for you."

Arthur removed the pins from his mouth and his jaw dropped. "I beg your pardon. I am the weirdest of all."

Chloe's dance partner, Paulo, looked over his shoulder. "You and Drew have been living together for three years, Arthur. He works in finance and you've adopted three rescue dogs. You're like the most stable person I know."

Chloe nodded. "I'm afraid it's true."

Arthur narrowed his eyes. "Take it back. Both of you."

Paulo continued, "Chloe, on the other hand, has a part-time not-relationship with her mysterious, hot boss, and I'm pretty sure she's sleeping with both her other roommates. She makes the rest of us look boring."

She put her head in her hands. "I'm not sleeping with either of my roommates."

Paulo rolled his eyes. "Then you're an idiot. 'Cause I've seen 'em."

"Agreed." Arthur started pinning the seams of the flowing shirt Paulo would wear over his flesh-toned tank top. The burgundy color would be stunning against Paulo's light brown skin and shoulder-length black hair.

Chloe and Paulo were only one of five pairs of dancers who would be performing three new contemporary dance pieces at the theater on the Lower East Side. Far from the simple, skintight minimalism shown in most modern dance, this time the choreographer had asked for flowing costumes that almost resembled feathers.

The choreographer was a personal friend of Arthur's, which was the only reason Chloe'd even had a chance to audition. They were rehearsing at a shared space on 8th Avenue, and they had just four weeks until the performance. They had one weekend to make an impression, but she was hoping it could be a break.

It wasn't what Chloe had dreamed of when she first moved to New York, but then what was? She'd thought she'd work her way up to Broadway; instead, she hooked up with a narcissist who tried to crush her spirit and keep her just low enough to always need his help.

The new show was her first real opportunity to shine again. She felt like she was getting her life back on track. Her confidence was growing. She was making things happen, not just reacting when life happened to her.

So why was she allowing herself to second-guess what she and Gavin shared?

"I'm overreacting," she told Arthur. "Everyone has off nights. Everyone gets stressed out sometimes."

"Even Tenzin?"

"Tenzin is the exception to most rules," she muttered.

"Okay, baby, you're done." Arthur smacked Paulo's butt and sent him on his way. "Don't let me catch you calling me normal again. And tell Carrie I'm ready for her."

Paulo gave them both a shake of his hips before he walked back to the floor. "Carreeeeeee!"

Chloe smiled at the easy camaraderie between her fellow dancers. She was a couple of years older than most of them, but they still made her feel welcome even though it was her first show in two years.

"Joking aside," Arthur said. "The minute you feel that man trying to make you smaller or duller or anything that feels less *you*, get out. Do you hear me?" He leaned forward. "I like what I know of Gavin. And I like the people he calls his friends. But you're too precious and too bright to let anyone do that to you. I could not bear to lose you again, and you always know you have a spot on our couch if you need it."

Chloe tried not to let any tears come to her eyes. "Your dogs own your couch, Arthur."

"Oh, shut up." He pulled out a blue shift. "Carrie, get your blond butt over here!"

Chloe laughed. "But the dogs might let me have the horrible recliner."

He curled his lip. "Yes, because they are my babies and they know how awful that thing is."

"You can take the boy out of the Midwest..."

"But he'll still inherit his grandfather's taste in furnishings." Arthur rolled his eyes. "Trust me, I know."

"You think I'm overreacting to Gavin being weird?"

"No." He turned the shift inside out and dropped it over the tiny blonde who came running over. "I think you should trust your instincts. If you think he's hiding something, he's probably hiding something."

"I don't think..." Chloe stopped herself.

Actually, Gavin *did* seem like he was hiding something. The problem with dating—or not dating?—a vampire was you had no idea if the secret the person was concealing was for your own good or just a shitty, human-type secret.

It was possible that Gavin knew about some serious threat that jeopardized the immortal population of New York City. It was also possible he wanted to break up with her and didn't want to hurt her feelings.

No, that wouldn't be it. Gavin was blunt almost to the point of cruelty at times. If there was something he wanted to tell her, he'd just tell her. Which meant...

"I think this is something that has nothing to do with me," she said. "I'm probably overreacting. I should be more supportive."

"Totally," Arthur said. "Lend the man an ear if he needs it. From what you've told me, he probably has a million people depending on him. He might just need a safe place to vent about something."

"Yeah." Chloe nodded. "You're right."

"I'll be honest. I don't understand your relationship, but the man has had the patience of Job"—Arthur raised a pair of scissors—"which of course he should have, because you needed time and you're worth every damn minute."

"You're totally worth it," Carrie said. "I have no idea what's going on, but you're awesome, Chloe."

"Thanks, Carrie. You're the sweetest."

Arthur continued, "So we know Gavin has patience and he cares about you a lot, because he's not an idiot. Also, he's very, very hot for you. Because the eyes that man gives you when you're not looking make me..." Arthur fanned his face. "It's hot. So very hot."

Carrie looked over her shoulder. "Can I meet him? I want to meet him."

Chloe shook her head, but Arthur said, "Go to the Dancing Bear. That new pub on 9th. Super fun. It's where she works, and the hot Scottish guy is her boss."

"Ooooh. Illicit. Also, accent."

"And kilts sometimes."

Carrie's eyes went wide. "For real?"

"It's not..." Chloe put her head in her hands. "Yes. He wears kilts sometimes."

"Because he knows she likes them," Arthur whispered a little too loudly. "Plus he's rich."

Carrie made a face.

Chloe said, "But not from a trust fund."

"Oh, nice." Carrie nodded. "So what time does the bar close?"

"Three," Arthur said. "And tonight I think we're all going."

Gavin eyed the group of dancers Chloe waved at as they came in. He recognized a few of them, and he definitely recognized Arthur even though the small man's hair was a completely new shade of violet.

Which suited his eyes, actually. Gavin would have to

compliment him when they had a chance to speak.

Arthur was a good enough friend to Chloe that he put up with the rather raucous crowd he attracted every time he visited the pub. Gavin couldn't complain that they monopolized her, especially when they bought so many drinks.

Besides, he was meeting with Cormac that night.

"As far as I know, Vivian Lebeau has never visited my city before," Cormac said. "Can I expect this... pleasure to be more frequent now that you're a resident?"

Gavin grimaced. "Vivian is impossible to predict, and I haven't seen her in over twenty years. So I wish I could tell you, Cormac. I honestly do. But I can't."

Cormac cast his eyes toward Chloe. "Does she know about...?"

"No, and if possible, I'd like to avoid the two of them ever meeting. It wouldn't go well for either."

"You've made your attachment clear," Cormac said. "It's none of my business, and I won't say anything, but I don't think she's going to avoid the rumors about your relationship."

"What rumors?" Gavin's spine stiffened.

Cormac cocked his head. "The rumors that Gavin Wallace has found a human paramour. The rumors that he intends to steal her from Giovanni Vecchio's aegis. The rumors that he's so attached he might even ask Vecchio to turn her."

Gavin could say nothing, because those were all thoughts he'd entertained at some point over the previous year. Oh, not *Vecchio* turning Chloe. He had someone else in mind for that. But keeping her for himself? Yes. Stealing her from Giovanni's aegis and putting her under his own? Absolutely.

"I'd appreciate your discretion," Gavin said. "If I can keep Vivian from knowing the extent of our relationship, I know you'd agree that it would be best for everyone."

"I've never met Vivian, but I know her reputation." Cormac took a long breath and let it out slowly. "I like Chloe. She's also impressed people who are important to me. She's a gifted human and a valuable member of Giovanni's aegis. So you can be assured that as long as she's in *my* city, she's under *my* protection. Is that clear enough?"

"Will you make that clear to others, should it become necessary?"

"If you think that will help."

"Thank you, Cormac." Gavin glanced at Chloe from the secluded table. It must be her break time, because she was taking a tray of drinks to Arthur's table while Rafael watched the bar. "Protection offered to Chloe Reardon will garner you a favor from me."

Cormac's eyebrows rose. "I didn't ask for one."

"I offered anyway."

The corner of Cormac's mouth turned up in a crooked smile. "Well, well, well. If you ask me, it sounds like the rumors are true."

"Is he looking over here?" Chloe murmured to Arthur.

"He can't keep his eyes off you. Who's the character with him?"

"Oh, that's Cormac. Whiskey distributor." The lie

tripped easily off her tongue. Of course, it helped that Cormac did distribute whiskey. He also had a bourbon distillery in Kentucky. And he was the head vampire in charge of New York City, but Arthur didn't need to know that.

"Ah, he's got that hipster look, doesn't he? Is that..." Arthur squinted. "Is he actually wearing a pocket watch? Unironically?"

"Yes, he's wearing it, but I can't judge the irony," Chloe said. "The irony is more your department than mine."

"You know..." Arthur cocked his head. "I dig it. The tweed, the combat boots. He makes it work. Not many could, and I think the facial hair helps."

Chloe nearly spit out the cider she was drinking. "I'll let him know."

"You should. My taste is impeccable."

"I love the new hair, by the way."

"Thanks." Arthur beamed. "I dyed it especially for Drew's company party two weeks ago. The purple color is exactly the same shade as the CEO's first wife's hair, who's also on the board and insists on coming to the parties even though she was replaced by wife number two twenty years ago."

"And how does the second wife feel about the first wife showing up to company parties?"

"Oh, she's long gone." Arthur waved his hand. "She was replaced two times over. I think he's on number four."

Chloe shook her head. Anyone who thought vampire relationships were weird didn't know enough rich humans. "Gavin has been busy tonight. I've barely had time to talk to him. Of course, it is Thursday." Thursday nights were always insanely busy for them. Chloe had no idea why. Everyone was ready for the end of the week, but not quite as exhausted as on Friday, she guessed.

"Judging from the serious looks on both their gruff, manly faces, I'd say your man and his buddy Cormac have some serious business shit going on. I'll bet you twenty that whatever is going on with him is related to work."

Chloe took a long breath. "You're probably right."

"Of course I am. Now get me another martini, woman."

Three nights later, Chloe still didn't have any answers. Gavin had locked himself in his office most nights at the bar, he'd been affectionate but distant when they interacted, and Chloe had made excuses to stay at Ben and Tenzin's loft every night since Wednesday.

Usually Gavin argued with her when she did that. He'd tell her his place was closer to work. He'd insist on taking a car late at night, then try to make her feel guilty about Abe driving all the way to SoHo. He'd offer to cook dinner for her—he was an excellent cook—then feed her so much she fell into a food coma at his house.

But in the four nights since he'd left her in the hot tub and come back a different man, he'd done none of those things. He was distracted. He was distant. And Chloe felt herself shrinking back.

This is how it starts.

This is where the end begins.

Her heart hurt, and Chloe was glad she'd held off having sex with him. That took a whole new level of trust for her since Tom, one she didn't want to share with just anyone.

Gavin wasn't just anyone.

Wrong. He might be an immortal, but he was also just another man. And Chloe had learned the hard way that most of them couldn't be trusted.

On Thursday night, she'd brought a bag to work, thinking that Gavin might ask her to stay over. It had remained in her locker since then. On Sunday night, the bar closed at one in the morning. Chloe decided to take the bag back to SoHo. Ben and Tenzin were gone and the loft felt empty, but she'd left a new paperback in the bag and she really wanted to start it.

By the time she realized the book wasn't in her bag, she was already on the train.

"Dammit."

Did she need the book? She had others at the loft. She'd been really excited to start it though. The bar was closed on Monday, and she didn't want to wait two days.

She let out a long breath and got off at the next stop. Maybe she could just hire a car to take her home. Maybe a ride share. She trudged back uptown and over to 9th Avenue, glad she at least had keys and didn't have to call Gavin.

Since it was only one thirty, plenty of bars were still open on 9th, so she didn't feel alone. A few of the bouncers waved at her and Chloe waved back. She opened the street door and walked up the stairs, instinctively listening for any movement in the pub. She heard nothing.

She flipped on the overhead lights but halted just inside the entrance.

Gavin was still there. But he wasn't alone.

He was standing at the bar in his shirtsleeves, suit jacket draped over a barstool, sipping whiskey from his favorite glass.

Sitting across from him at the bar was a beautiful woman with a complexion so perfectly white Chloe knew she had to be a vampire. She was wearing a sleeveless black evening gown, and her hair fell in shiny auburn waves down her back.

The woman turned to look at her, a single eyebrow arched. "I thought we were going out for dinner, *mon loup*. Did you order delivery instead?"

"Chloe," Gavin said, sounding indifferent, "can I help you?"

Her throat dried up. She could feel her pulse pounding through her body. Her voice sounded tiny when she spoke. "I left a book in my locker."

No reaction. Nothing. He stared at her as if they barely knew each other. "Very well. The break room should be open."

She shook her head. "Fine." She started to back out of the room. "It's fine. I don't need it."

Don't need you.

Never you.

Never this.

She managed to back out the door and walk halfway down the stairs before the tears began to fall. Her heart felt like an icepick had been shoved through it. Cold rain hit her face the minute she walked out the door.

Chloe didn't stop. She kept walking. All she cared about was getting away.

4

Fuck, fuck, fuck, fuck. Gavin couldn't allow his emotions show on his face, not with Vivian around. He turned to her and shrugged. "She's my manager. Must not have wanted to interrupt."

Vivian smirked. "Seems like a skittish little thing."

"Humans." He sipped his whiskey and kept his voice even and calm. "Who knows what their motivations are."

"I recall hearing that you'd become quite close with that human boy of Giovanni Vecchio's. Would you call him a friend?"

"Ben?" Gavin walked around the bar, resisting the urge to follow Chloe out the door, and sat next to Vivian at the bar. "Ben Vecchio is an immortal in everything but biology. He thinks like us, acts like us—it's hardly the same thing." *Find a way to turn it around to her.* "What about you? How are your human employees these days? Have the economic problems in France affected your operation?"

"Not in the least. We're quite insulated from all that. You know how I take care of my people."

Vivian took care of her people in the same way feudal lords took care of their serfs. She assumed they adored her, patronized them, then used them however she liked. Gavin had to admit she paid better than a feudal lord though, which was why Vivian inspired loyalty among her staff even if she didn't inspire love.

"So what's going on?" Gavin said. "Why are you here?"

"Can't I just come for a visit?"

"No."

She pouted. "You're very cross this evening."

"I'm very cross every evening, Vivi. You've known me longer than anyone else. This shouldn't be a surprise."

What was Chloe doing? Was she taking the train? Hiring a car? Gavin heard the rain outside. Was it safe to be driving in this kind of rain?

"My new winemaker has had an intriguing idea about our brandy-distilling process, and I wanted to explore it," Vivian said.

"Oh?"

Chloe had to get all the way to SoHo in this weather. Gavin wondered if he should call his driver. Abraham had her number.

"Yes, bourbon is quite trendy in Europe at the moment," Vivian continued, "and Albert thinks importing used casks to age some of our spirits might be an interesting experiment."

Would she even pick up if Abe called? Dammit, why was tomorrow Monday? He had no excuse to see her for over forty-eight hours.

And why the fuck was Vivian still talking?

"I've heard that Cormac O'Brien produces some of the best bourbon in the United States. I knew you were living here now. So I thought you could make the introduction."

Gavin cut his eyes toward her. "Cormac's bourbon casks are in high demand, Vivian. Your distiller is behind the curve. I don't think there's a whiskey barrel in Bourbon County that isn't spoken for these days. Brewers are using them for beer, winemakers are buying them, distilleries all over the world have them on order."

"Well, surely he could spare a few for an old friend—"

"Don't make the mistake of thinking we're friends, Vivian." Gavin turned to her.

"Who?" she asked. "You and me? Or you and O'Brien?"

"Either. Cormac allows me in this city because we have an arrangement that suits us both. As for you and me—"

"We're more than friends." Vivian sipped her drink. "I know."

"You know nothing," Gavin growled. "And you're not being honest with me. And I'm losing patience."

She shrugged. "You're always cross when I visit. You should have stayed in Ireland with Deirdre. She made you... Well, not happy, but less cross."

The mention of Deirdre stung, just like Vivian had intended. "Deirdre and I weren't meant to be. Drop it."

"But I liked her." Vivian leaned her chin on her perfectly manicured hand. "The two of you had very volatile chemistry. Was the sex good? I'm guessing it was."

"Be quiet, Vivi." Gavin set his glass down on the bar to keep from strangling her. "Deirdre lost her mate. You don't get over that in a few years."

She curled her lip. "And that is why our kind should never mate. Such a foolish practice."

I'm sure it is for you. "Why are you here?"

"For bourbon casks."

"You're lying." He stood. "And I've lost my patience. I have things to do that don't involve you. Veronica will settle you in your rooms at the penthouse. Time for you to go." He gestured to the door.

Vivian stood and picked up her fur wrap. "I thought we were going out to dinner."

"Do whatever you want to do." Gavin ushered her toward the door. "I've lost my appetite."

CHLOE STARED AT HER PHONE, trying to process what she was supposed to do next.

Should she call someone? It was two thirty in the morning. She couldn't call anyone she wanted to talk to. She nearly called Tenzin, knowing that the vampire didn't sleep at all, but then she decided against it. Tenzin was on a job. And she was out of the country. It wasn't her job to fix Chloe's problems.

Sleep? She couldn't sleep. She didn't even want to change her clothes. She kept remembering the last time she'd worn the shirt she was wearing tonight. It was the week before, and Gavin had made a point to run his fingers across her shoulders and arms because he liked the velvet softness of the material so much. Or maybe he just liked touching her.

She thought he had liked touching her.

Tonight he hadn't touched her. He hadn't even looked at her. He'd looked *through* her.

Can I help you?

So cold. So distant.

It was past two in the morning and Chloe was soaked to the skin, but she liked the numbness. She had this horrible fear that the minute she got into the shower and warmed up, she would start hurting again. The pain in her chest had receded the farther she'd walked in the cold. She'd caught a cab near the playground where Ben practiced parkour and paid too much for the old man in the cab to just get her back to SoHo.

And now she was home, staring at her phone, and she didn't know what she was supposed to do.

The phone buzzed, and Gavin's name and picture flashed on the screen.

Chloe dropped it, and the device fell between her feet and onto the hardwood floor of the loft. She heard something crack.

Shit.

The phone kept buzzing, but she didn't touch it.

Water pooled on the ground, seeping from her soaked shoes. She stood, walked to the door, and left her boots on the rack Tenzin insisted on. Tenzin hated for anyone to wear shoes in the loft. Chloe took off her jacket and hung it on the hooks. It was dripping too.

The phone buzzed in the background.

Again. Someone was calling again.

Who was the vampire at the bar? A lover? A business associate?

If Gavin hadn't been distant for days, Chloe wouldn't

have assumed the worst. She would have assumed there was some explanation. If Gavin hadn't been cold, she would have assumed it was just another aspect of vampire life she was blissfully ignorant about.

Isn't that part of the problem?

She walked downstairs with her phone still buzzing on the floor. She walked straight to the newly renovated bathroom and turned on the hot water in the shower as she stripped off the rest of her damp clothes.

It was never going to work. Better that you face the truth now.

Who was the vampire?

It didn't matter. Not really. The fact that Gavin couldn't or wouldn't tell her what was bothering him—which likely had something to do with the vampire at the bar—was the point.

Chloe wasn't a part of his world. She'd been dipping her toes in the water, but she was never going to be brave enough to dive in.

She stepped under the hot spray and let the water beat against her skin, driving the numbness away as tears fell down her cheeks. They washed down her body with the grit and grime of the city, slipping between her toes before they vanished in the darkness.

Why was it so dark?

She'd forgotten to turn on the lights in the bathroom. Only the dim glow from the hallway illuminated the shower.

That was fine. She didn't need the fluorescent white glare. She washed her hair, conditioned it, and rinsed it. She'd wrap it before she went to bed. She wasn't going anywhere tomorrow. She didn't plan on seeing anyone. Not Gavin. Not anyone.

The towels tucked into the cubbies were Tenzin's favorites. Turkish peshtemal, thin cotton wraps that were surprisingly comfortable. She dried off her body and wrapped the towel around herself before she walked to her room.

She slipped on a pair of leggings and an oversized sweater that fell nearly to her knees. It was one of Ben's that she'd stolen.

She wished Ben was here. She wished Arthur was awake. Maybe she'd take Arthur up on his offer of a couch, at least for a few days.

Chloe wrapped a scarf around her hair and knotted the ends on top of her head. She sat on the edge of her bed and wondered again what she was supposed to do.

Call someone? Who would she call? What would even be the point?

Sleep?

Impossible.

There was a noise in the distance. A neighbor? That was strange. They never heard neighbors on the top floor.

No, not a neighbor.

Chloe walked out of her room and toward the stairs.

Someone was banging on the door. Not the front door—no one could get up the elevator without a special code—but the glass door to the roof garden.

"Chloe!"

Her eyes went wide.

"Chloe Reardon, I can see your phone on the ground. I know you're here."

Chloe moved from sad to angry in a blink. She marched up the stairs and across the living room. Gavin was standing at the french doors, as soaked as she'd been. His perfectly pressed shirt was sticking to his skin, and wet hair hung in his eyes.

"Go away."

He pointed at her phone. "No. Fuck that. We need to talk and you're not answering your phone."

"I know! Get a clue."

"Will you please let me in?"

"Go away."

"I want to explain."

"Explain what?" Chloe felt the heat of anger in her cheeks. "Did she send you for take-out once delivery walked out the door?"

He clenched his jaw. "That's not what this is about. Will you please let me in?"

Chloe's voice was shaking with anger. "I'm pretty sure there are servers at the Bat and Barrel who get paid extra for that. Talk to them, because I'm not on the menu."

"Will you stop?" He banged on the glass. "Vivian is my sister, and she's a wee radge! D'ye think I want her knowing how much I care about ye? D'ye think that would end well, Chloe?"

Her stomach dropped, and the flush of anger turned to embarrassment. "Your sister?"

"Yes! My mad-as-snakes older sibling. Will you *please* let me in?"

Chloe didn't know what to say. Or do. She still didn't want to talk to Gavin, but she didn't have a good reason anymore. He'd called her multiple times. He was trying to explain. He'd flown through the rain to get there.

It was never going to work. Better to end things now.

Gavin leaned his head against the glass, water running down the window around him. "Chloe," he said plaintively, "let me in. Please."

She unlocked the french doors, her stomach tied in knots, and allowed him into the apartment.

He walked toward her before he paused. "Yer dry and I'm drookit and I want to hold ye, but I dinnae want to get ye wet and cold."

She held up a hand. "It's better... Just stay here. I'll get you a towel."

Chloe walked downstairs and retrieved one of the plush towels from the hall closet along with a Turkish towel from the bathroom. She walked back upstairs to find Gavin, barefoot and shirtless, still standing by the french doors.

Don't look. You know he's not for you.

Chloe handed him the towels, then she turned back to the living room couch and sat down, picking up her phone and setting it on the coffee table. She refused to look at Gavin while he undressed.

He is not for you.

"You cracked your screen." Gavin rubbed a towel through his hair. He'd taken off his trousers and wrapped the peshtemal around his waist. "Was that tonight?"

She scooted down the couch and Gavin sat next to her, keeping some distance between them. "I dropped it when you called."

"I'll buy you a new one."

She shook her head. "Not necessary."

"It's my own fault."

"I drop my phone all the time, Gavin. I can get this one fixed."

"It's old. You should have a new one. Between work and rehearsal—"

"I'm not..." She took a deep breath. "I think it's better if I don't work at the pub anymore. I'll come in long enough for you to find a replacement, but—"

"What?" His voice went cold. "Yer bum's oot the windae."

Chloe let out a breath, trying to keep herself from tearing up.

It was never going to work. He is not for you.

"Don't make this impossible," she whispered.

"I told ye, Vivian is my sister. Nothing is going on between us. She's a complication. She shows up every few years and wreaks a bit of havoc before she flies off again. I'm trying to explain—"

"The problem is, I don't want to know." She swallowed the lump in her throat. "Don't you see, Gavin? That's always been the problem. That's why we haven't been able to move forward."

His chin jutted out. "Ye want me, and I want ye. Ye just need time. I'm giving ye time. I'm not some randy lad—"

"Gavin"—her voice cracked—"this was never going to work."

The silence from him was deafening.

"You can't be in a relationship with someone when you actively avoid knowing about their life. You need to know all of them. Not just parts." Chloe plowed on, even as the tears started to form in her eyes. "It's not your fault. It's me.

I'm not Ben. I'm not... Veronica even. You don't tell me things—"

"I'm *trying* to tell ye things. I'm trying to explain."

"And I'm telling you I don't want to know." She felt the tears slip away from her. "I'm not built for this. I'm not brave."

"Fuck yes, ye are. Ye *are*."

"I'm not. At first it was exciting. But every night it gets deeper and deeper. And I'm not built for this. I'm not looking for adventure like Ben and Tenzin. I just... After everything that's already happened, I want— I *need* to be safe."

He angled his body toward her. "And ye don't think I can keep ye safe?"

Chloe didn't know what to say.

Gavin slipped off the couch and knelt before her. He put his hand on her cheek and forced her eyes to his. His gaze locked on hers. "Do ye believe I can keep ye safe, Chloe Reardon?"

She blinked away tears. "I don't know."

He wasn't angry. His fingers were soft on her skin. His eyes were wide open, penetrating the thick wall of resolve she'd tried to erect. She tried to be immune to him, the hard planes of his chest, the vibrating energy she felt coming off him.

She wasn't successful.

"No," he said. "Ye dinnae know, and that's my own fault. Maybe I should have made ye look more closely, forced ye to see all of me." His voice hardened. "I've spent many years acquiring wealth and influence. Very powerful people owe me favors, and I'm very stingy about using them.

But know this, Chloe Reardon, I protect the people I care about. The people who work for me are untouchable because I'm very smart and very strategic about the alliances I make. And when it comes to *you*?"

Her heart stopped when Gavin took her chin in his fingers and tilted her mouth to his.

"There is *nothing* I wouldn't do to keep ye safe."

Gavin kissed her like it was the first time and the last time. He took her breath away. His lips moved against hers, searching for surrender. She opened her mouth to him, and he swallowed her needy cry.

He reached out, grabbing her hips and dragging her toward the edge of the couch, forcing her to grip his shoulders. Her fingers dug in, pressing him closer.

A low, guttural moan came from his throat as he drove his tongue into her mouth. Chloe felt the edge of his fangs nick her flesh and tasted the blood he craved. The hands at her hips moved back, cupping her bottom as he drew her closer.

She slid off the couch and onto his lap, riding the hard line of the erection jutting underneath the thin cotton wrap. Gavin's hand gripped the back of her neck, his fingers playing with the curls that escaped her scarf. His arms were like iron around her, but nothing about them caged her. She didn't feel crushed or wary. She felt... free.

Maybe it wouldn't work out in the end. Maybe it would all come crashing down. But for tonight she needed him. She wanted him so much it hurt.

She pulled her mouth from his. "Take me to bed," she said against his cheek.

"Yes." He stood, and Chloe wrapped her legs around his waist. "We have to lock the doors."

"Cara, lock roof doors," Chloe yelled.

A polite, robotic voice answered back, "Locking roof doors. It is 3:17 a.m. Engage nighttime security protocol?"

"Yes."

"Nighttime security protocol active until sunrise."

Gavin muttered, "I really need to install one of these systems."

"Can we talk about that later?"

"Yes, but before we go downstairs..." Gavin set her on her feet.

"What are you doing?"

"Just this." He reached down and gripped the edge of her sweater before he pulled it up and over her head. "Tossing that." He threw it across the room. "Much better." His hands ran down her shoulders and cupped her small breasts before he lifted her again. "I could smell him on ye, and it was irritating."

"You're such a vampire."

"Yes, I am." Gavin lifted her higher and licked over the rise of her left breast. "Fuck, it's pure dead brilliant." He sucked her nipple into his mouth and nipped her with his teeth. "So fucking sweet."

Chloe watched him, and she couldn't stop the moan that left her throat. Watching Gavin put his mouth on her was incredibly hot. "Bed," she said. "Please."

"Yes." He walked them down the stairs to her bedroom. Gavin tossed her on the bed and reached down to the edge of her leggings. "These have to go."

"Are you going to bite me?" Her heart pounded.

Gavin smiled a wicked grin as he stripped the thin leggings from her body. "Let's not get ahead of ourselves, dove. Plenty to do tonight." His mouth dropped open and his fangs fell as he ran both his hands up the outside of her thighs. "Look at ye. Those legs are fucking works of art."

"Light," she whispered, overcome with sensation. She felt him. She heard him. She wanted to see him too.

Gavin laid her legs down on the bed. Then he reached over and switched on the lamp at her bedside. He loosened the towel around his waist and let the cloth drop.

He was magnificent. His body was lean and defined. His erection jutted out above muscled thighs. Chloe reached over and drew him to her mouth, tasting and teasing him.

As she played with his erection and he let out a long and highly imaginative stream of curses, he reached up and untied the knot holding her hair back.

Chloe stopped and reached up. "What are you doing?"

"You weren't supposed to stop." He gripped the base of his erection. "But if you're curious, I have had roughly a thousand fantasies regarding sex with you, and in none of them is your hair wrapped up."

"It's a mess, Gavin."

"Don't care." His fingers teased out the wet curls as he tossed her scarf over the side of the bed. "I want it. I want you."

They could talk about the realities of hair later. "Come here."

"Hmmm. Not quite yet." He sat on the edge of the bed and swung her leg over his head. His fangs were long and he was grinning. "You had a taste of me, dove. Turnabout is fair play."

Chloe felt her cheeks flush. "I thought you weren't going to bite me."

"That's not the kind of taste I'm talking about." He slid off the bed, knelt in front of her, and ran his fangs up the inside of her thigh. "This is what I've been craving." He nipped the inside of her thigh once before he put his mouth on her and feasted.

Chloe let out a harsh cry as Gavin worked. He held her ass and lifted, forcing her back into an arch. It didn't take long for her to climax. Her body was primed by months and months of foreplay.

"Fuck!" She tugged his hair and held him to her body. "Gavin!"

"That's the best kind of headache, dove, but you'd better let me up." He laughed against her thigh and gave her pussy one more lick, making her body shudder. "There's someone who very much wants to say hello."

"Please." She was out of breath, her skin shivering.

"The best please I've ever heard," Gavin whispered, crawling up her body and holding himself over her. "Chloe, look at me."

She couldn't look anywhere else. In that moment, he was everything. She was wet and wanting, swollen with desire for him. Chloe dug her fingers into his shoulders and looked straight into his eyes. "Please, Gavin."

"Yes." His voice was rough. "Worth every second of the wait."

He slid inside and Chloe wrapped her legs around his

waist, pulling him closer. The pressure was intense, but so pleasurable she felt light-headed.

"Chloe."

"Yeah?" She could barely speak. He felt so good. So right.

"Don't close yer eyes."

She opened them and watched every piece of his armor fall away. Gavin's lips were flushed and full with desire. His eyes watched her as he bucked his hips forward, making her mouth fall open in ecstasy.

"What do ye feel right now?"

"You." She put her hands on his cheeks and drew him down for a kiss. "All of you."

"And I feel ye." His eyes turned fierce. "I will keep ye safe, Chloe Reardon. And we *will* make this work."

There were no more words after that. There were soft sighs and harsh gasps. Hands gripping. The delicious, heavy weight of his body on hers. Electricity across her skin, and heat. So much heat.

When he came, he whispered her name. Just her name. And it was everything.

5

Gavin lay next to Chloe while she slept. He'd never been more satisfied by a sexual encounter. Even though she was human and he'd had to be careful not to harm her, she was extraordinary. It was possible that the feeling was a result of Gavin abstaining for over a year, but it was more likely because he'd never had sex with a woman he was in love with.

He was in love with Chloe.

And he was going to be an absolute nightmare.

Gavin wanted to lock her in a bulletproof bunker. He wanted to cart her off to his apartment, lock her inside, and kill anyone who came close to her. His territorial instincts were in overdrive, and his apartment wasn't safe because Vivian was there.

The loft was safe—he knew logically this was the best place for her—but Ben's and Tenzin's scents were everywhere. He didn't want to leave her here.

What other safe houses did he own?

Los Angeles? Too far away.

Houston? Also too far.

The inaccessible cabin in the Poconos? A much better option.

But not practical for the moment. It took two hours to fly to the cabin, and he only had an hour before dawn.

He should be leaving.

He should leave her at the loft, knowing that Ben and Tenzin's security was highly sophisticated, and he should take shelter during the day in his apartment, which was only a short flight away. He had plenty of time.

But he didn't want to leave.

Gavin watched her, languidly draped over his body, her breath warm against his skin.

Impossible.

This was never going to work.

I'm not brave.

I need *to be safe.*

Gavin had panicked. He'd felt her slipping away like smoke on the wind. He couldn't lose her, not when he'd finally realized what she meant. But he'd made a mistake with Chloe. He'd assumed that if he showed her who he truly was, she'd run. He'd tried to make himself safe, and in doing so had made her question his ability to protect her.

It wasn't a mistake an immortal would make, but Chloe wasn't an immortal.

He played with a curl of her hair. His hands and the sheets had turned it into a mess, but he didn't care. He loved it. He'd wash it for her the next night. He'd been dying to put his hands in it for months.

Chloe shifted on his chest, and Gavin moved with her, unwilling to break his hold.

You're going to be an utter nightmare, and she is wholly unprepared for it.

There was a reason his employees were safe, a reason that Chloe would be as well. Gavin was a businessman, and violence was bad for business. No one pissed off Gavin Wallace without suffering the consequences of banishment from his pubs or—if you truly pissed him off—a silent and untraceable death. Of course, it took a lot to make him that angry.

Gavin was Switzerland, a consistent neutral party in a world of constantly shifting allegiances. He had very few friends, most of whom were politically neutral, and very few loyalties to anyone who didn't pay him. He was predictable, steady, and only looked out for the small group of people who were his employees.

And Chloe.

Keeping her and Vivian apart was still a priority, but there would be no way of hiding his attachment from the greater immortal world, not if he wanted them to keep their distance. But could Gavin ease her into a relationship while shielding her from the true breadth of his feelings until she was ready for them?

His mind was a riot of contradictions.

He slid out of bed and wrapped a towel around his waist. The first hurdle was negotiating territories, so he called Tenzin.

She picked up the phone in seconds. "What's wrong with Chloe?"

"She's safe, but I need to use the light-safe room at your loft."

"Why?"

"Because I don't want to leave her."

"I thought you said she was safe."

"She is."

A long pause.

"You finally had sex with her."

"Tenzin—"

"I'm very relieved. You'll need to inform Giovanni."

Gavin saw red. "I'm not fucking informing the Italian about my sex life, Tenzin. If he thinks otherwise—"

"She's under his aegis. You'll have to make some kind of statement soon."

Fuck, fuck, fuck! Tenzin was correct.

Gavin clenched his jaw. "Fine. I'll... inform him; I'm not asking permission."

"He knows about your relationship. I can't imagine he'll be surprised. Though he does have very paternal feelings toward her, so be prepared for that."

"Fuck you. I just called to let you know I'm here."

"Do you want me to tell Benjamin?"

"That Chloe and I are having sex? Of course not. It's none of his fucking business."

"Fine." She hung up. Typical.

Gavin knew where the light-safe guest quarters were in Ben and Tenzin's loft. They were spacious, comfortable, and secure. He could rest easy, knowing that he'd be safe during his day rest.

But only if he had guards on Chloe.

He called the bodyguard he'd used for Chloe in the

past. "Audra?"

"Yeah, boss, what's up?"

She didn't comment about the hour. He tried to respect his employees' time, so if Gavin called in the middle of the night, they knew it was important. "I need you to guard Chloe today."

Audra's voice immediately grew sharper. "Threats?"

"No."

"Special circumstances?"

"Not really."

"Where will she be going?"

"I'm honestly not sure. She's not scheduled to work. Be available at the loft." He could tell from the silence that the normally unflappable Audra was a bit confused. "Just... consider yourself assigned to her for the foreseeable future."

"You got it, boss. I'll be there by sunrise."

"Thank you."

Gavin hung up the phone. Was he being an asshole? Possibly. Did he care? No.

He went back to the bedroom and knelt next to her. He needed to lock himself in a light-safe room. The sky out her window was already touched with pearl grey.

He didn't want to leave.

"Chloe."

"Hmm." She rolled over, the sheet draped over her perfect breasts.

They truly were perfect. Or he was a sentimental sop.

No, they were perfect.

"Chloe, I have to leave."

Her eyes flickered open, and she gave him a sleepy smile. "Hey."

The smile caused his dead heart to thump. "Hey."

She blinked and looked at the window. "You're still here."

"I didn't want to lock myself in without saying good morning."

She wrinkled her forehead. "Are you staying here?"

"If you don't mind."

Chloe smiled again. "No, I don't mind. That means I'll get to see you at sunset." She stretched and the sheet slipped down.

Gavin's fangs dropped. "I really don't want to leave you right now, but I'm going to appear mostly dead in roughly half an hour. I don't think you're quite ready for that bit yet."

She shook her head. "So weird."

"I'm actually the normal type for my kind. Tenzin is the weird one."

"So you'll be like... really, really asleep, huh?"

"Yes."

"Weird."

He reached over and pinched her bottom, eliciting a laughing shriek.

I love you. I adore you. You make me feel alive again.

"Did you have any plans today?" he asked, swallowing the other words that wanted to slip out.

She rolled over and curled up, pulling the sheet over her shoulders. "I was going to read my book. The one that caused all the drama. But I don't have it."

He shook his head. "I caused the drama. I should have told you about Vivian. In my defense, our relationship is strange, complicated, and unhealthy."

"Is she the one who called the other night?"

He nodded.

"Sister, huh?"

"Not in the familiar and somewhat affectionate manner of some families. Our sire wasn't the kind to foster familial relationships. Or relationships of any kind, really."

"What happened to him?"

"Someone killed him. Tellingly, neither Vivian nor I sought revenge. He crossed the wrong person and got what was coming to him. I took the money I got from him and refurbished a club in Hong Kong."

"Wow. So no hard feelings, huh?"

"None. It was a business matter that went wrong. If there's one thing that my sire taught me, it's that business is sacrosanct."

She reached up and traced the line of his eyebrow. "Is it?"

His heart thumped again. "My business is part of what will keep you safe, Chloe. So yes, for me it is sacrosanct."

A shadow fell over her eyes. "We still have a lot to talk about."

"We do." He leaned over and kissed her. "And we will talk more tonight when I'm not about to pass out and you've had time to relax and enjoy your well-deserved day off. Read a book. A different book. Take a nap. Relax."

"Sounds like a good plan."

"But please"—he kissed her again—"do not second-guess what happened last night. Last night was perfect."

Her cheeks flushed pleasantly. "It was pretty great."

"It was perfect." He could feel the first wave of dizziness wash over him. "But I have to go." Gavin leaned down and kissed her with all the tenderness he could muster when he still felt so territorial. "Go back to sleep. I'll see you at sunset."

CHLOE WATCHED him walk out of her bedroom, then she heard him open the door to the light-safe room past Ben's bedroom. It was spartan. More a vault than a bedroom. She heard the locks engage just as the first rays of dawn touched her window.

Was it her imagination, or did she feel colder?

At Gavin's apartment, Chloe never felt far from him, even during the day. His rooms were in the center of the house, away from all the windows, and the rest of the rooms surrounded him. He spent his days in the literal heart of the home. Whether that was by design or simply a quirk of architecture, Chloe found it comforting.

Here, in the cold, modern loft where vampires rarely slept, she felt like he'd disappeared.

Can you live like this? Because that's what he's asking for.

Chloe ignored the whispering voices in her mind and rolled over to replay the delicious memories of the night before.

Gavin had been... amazing.

Her skin felt electric. Just the memory of his hands on her body made her flush with heat. He was a thorough lover, indulging in every taste, every curve and corner of her body. He was... slightly obsessed with her legs. He hadn't pierced her skin, but her thighs and ankles had felt the blunt edge of his teeth. He'd devoured her and allowed her every liberty with his body too.

Months of wanting had given her plenty to imagine, and she had not been disappointed. His muscles weren't the defined, gym-and-protein-shake variety she was so accustomed to with male dancers. The men she worked with had the bodies of Greek gods, but they were work instruments. Nothing about them was attractive to her.

Gavin was strong—preternaturally strong—but his body wasn't made of hard lines. His skin was so pale he nearly glowed in the darkness. It was odd, but it was Gavin. Just the thought of him braced over her made Chloe smile.

She liked how his arms curved around her when he held her from behind and the contrast of his skin against hers. She liked the weight of his legs caging hers and the roughness of his feet when they tickled her ankles. He had several scars she wanted to ask about, one that looked like a bullet wound in his ass, and another few that marked his back and abdomen.

Even more than the sex, the tenderness after they'd made love was what stuck in her mind. He'd massaged every inch of her and run his fingers all over her body. Played with her hair—

"Ugh." Chloe put a hand in the unwieldy mass of curls that probably resembled something between a clown's wig and a tumbleweed. "That's not gonna be fun."

She refused to think about her hair. Not yet. Happy memories full in her mind, she put on some music and pulled the blankets up and over her deliciously well-used body.

Hours later, she heard her phone buzzing on the

bedside table. The sun was shining directly through her window when she sat up and rubbed her eyes. Picking up her phone—and grimacing at the cracked screen—she saw a message from Arthur.

Whatcha doing today?

She texted back. *Reading a new book.*

Boring. Come shopping for fabrics with me.

She cocked her head and frowned. Typical Arthur. *How is fabric shopping fun for me again?*

I'll make you something pretty! Shut up and come with me.

Chloe thought about Gavin's advice. She could stay in and relax or she could go shopping with Arthur. Part of her desperately wanted to chill out and replay everything that happened the night before, but the other part of her—

Come. Shopping. With. Me.

—the other part of her knew Arthur would pester her until she went shopping.

Fine. But I need to condition my hair, so I'm not dressing up.

Whatever. I'll look cute enough for both of us. Meet me at the bagel place at 10. Want. Coffee.

She sent a thumbs-up emoji and put her phone face-down. She needed to get going if she was going to meet Arthur at ten.

"Cara, play Happy Morning playlist."

"Good morning, Chloe. Cueing up Happy Morning playlist. It is 8:46 a.m. You have no voice messages this morning. Do you want a summary of the news today?"

"Most definitely not," she muttered.

"Very well. Playing Happy Morning playlist."

The sounds of fast guitar filled the loft, followed quickly by an electronic beat that set Chloe's heart beating faster. Music was an essential part of her life. She had playlists for everything: the morning, bedtime, practicing, stretching, grocery shopping. She was mentally composing a "Sex with Gavin" playlist in her head as she stepped in the warm spray of the shower. She wet her hair quickly and coated it with conditioner.

So much conditioner.

She was tapping her toes and moving to the beat when she remembered there was a huge, massive issue with going shopping with Arthur.

Gavin would be in the loft alone.

Was that okay? If they were at his place, she wouldn't think twice about leaving him in the apartment while she went about her daily routine. Why did it feel weird leaving Gavin at her place on his own when he was locked in the light-safe room?

"Huh." She blinked water out of her eyes. "I guess I *am* feeling territorial."

The thought made her want to giggle. She was the furthest thing from a vampire she could imagine, but she still felt weird leaving Gavin in Ben and Tenzin's territory without her presence.

She took a deep breath. "It's my house too."

Ben and Tenzin had always made that clear. This was Chloe's home. She wasn't a visitor. She wasn't couch surfing. This was her home. She helped pay the bills—what little she could—and she left her shoes by the door. She cooked and stocked the fridge.

And she could leave her vampire boyfriend in the vampire vault if she wanted to.

She shook her head. "Cara, how did my life get so weird?"

"I'm sorry, Chloe. I cannot answer that question."

"No, I don't think anyone can."

She rinsed her hair, turned off the water, and began the meticulous process of treating her hair with argan oil before she wrapped it again. She dressed in leggings and another long sweater, though this one was her own and not one she'd stolen from Ben.

She was grabbing her keys when a call came through the house system.

"Incoming video call from Beatrice De Novo."

Chloe stopped short of walking out the door. Ben's aunt rarely called the loft. And she had to know Ben was in Puerto Rico.

Weird.

"Accept call." She walked to the screen in the kitchen. "Hello?"

Ben's aunt appeared on the screen with a toddler in her lap. "Hey, Chloe."

"Hi!" Chloe grinned. "Hey, Sadia. How are you today?"

The toddler always looked suspicious. She sucked hard on a jewel-green pacifier, turned into her adoptive mother's shoulder, and hid her face.

"She's having a morning." Beatrice's hand ran over Sadia's curls. "I hope you don't mind me interrupting your day."

"I'm fine." She glanced out the windows. "How are you still awake?"

Chloe knew Beatrice didn't sleep much. Her father had been blood-bound to Tenzin before his death, which meant Beatrice and Tenzin shared some odd traits, including a very abbreviated sleep schedule. Normally, though, she'd be asleep at this hour.

"California time, remember? And Sadia wanted me, so I woke up. She couldn't sleep, so I don't either. Dad isn't quite as easy to wake up."

"Got it." Vampire families were weird. "What's up?"

"It's looking like we may need to head to the city in the next couple of days. I know Ben and Tenzin aren't there, but is it okay if Gio, Sadia, and I crash at the loft?"

"Uh..." *Sure. Just give me a night to move my vampire lover out of the safe room.* "Yeah, no problem."

"Are you sure?"

"Well, I'm assuming Gio will need the safe room. The bottom floor is all light safe except for the bedrooms, and Ben had shutters fitted in his room, so you and Sadia can probably stay in there. Uh..." She racked her brain to figure out the logistics. "The loft is *not* baby proofed. That's the only thing I can think that might be a problem."

"Don't worry about the baby proofing." Beatrice smiled. "I don't think she can reach Tenzin's sword collection yet. They're mounted pretty far up the wall. And we'll bring baby gates for the stairs." Her face brightened. "Oh! You haven't met Dema yet."

"Dema?" Who was Dema and where was she going to put another person? The futon in the training area was the other option, and it was hard as a rock.

"Yeah, Dema's our nanny slash bodyguard person. She's great. And she'll take care of all the baby-proofing stuff, so don't worry about that. Just give her a corner to crash and she'll be good."

"Are you sure?"

"She's ex-military. She's not picky."

Who got an ex-military nanny?

Vampires, that's who.

"Okay. If you're sure." Chloe glanced at her phone. "I'm running late to meet a friend, so I hope you don't mind—"

"No, that's cool!" Beatrice waved her hand. "Go. I just wanted to check. We were thinking Wednesday night, Thursday morning to arrive."

"Sure." This was going to get interesting. "And if you need more space, I can always stay at Gavin's."

Beatrice's smile went tight. "Right. Gavin. Sure."

What was it about Beatrice and Gavin? She didn't have time to mull it over. "I really have to go."

"We'll see you in a couple of days." She leaned over Sadia. "Do you want to wave bye?"

Sadia shook her head.

"Okay. Still having a morning." Beatrice lifted her hand to end the call. "See you soon, Chloe. Can't wait to hug you."

The screen went blank and Chloe rushed out the door. It was only after she found a seat on the train that she remembered that staying at Gavin's might not be as easy as it usually was.

After all, she wasn't the only one with company in town.

"Shit."

6

Chloe could tell when Arthur spotted her from the corner. He cocked his head and watched her approach, two large cups of coffee in his hands.

"Hey." She reached for the coffee.

"Hi." He held it out to her, then pulled it back. "You had sex."

Chloe blinked. "Wh-what?"

"You totally banged someone last night. It better have been Gavin, because that man needed to get some."

Chloe's mouth dropped open and she grabbed her coffee from his hand. "How could you possibly know—?"

"Women walk different after they have sex." He shrugged. "I've dressed thousands of you. I can tell."

"You cannot. You're making that up." She sipped her coffee. The temperature was perfect. "Thanks for getting the coffee."

"You're welcome." He hooked his arm in hers. "So... Gavin? I'm going to assume Gavin. You didn't deny it, and you haven't been making googly eyes at anyone else even though Lucas is totally into you."

"I'm not into Lucas, and I would never date a dancer I was in a show with. Do we have to talk about this?"

"About you finally banging your hot boss who's in love with you? Yes."

In love with me? Chloe's heart skipped a beat. "He's not... Gavin's not in love with me."

"Wrong!" Arthur crowed. "He is *so* in love with you. The way that man looks at you? He's in love."

Or he's hungry. It can be hard to tell with vampires. "Can we drop this please? It's all... new. And I just don't want to get overly— Look!" She pointed at a window. "Batik! Pretty."

"That's not batik. It's a damask. Don't try to distract me with things you know nothing about." Arthur glanced at the window. "Though... that is nice. It's thin, so it might drape —" He spun around and pointed at her. "You're evil."

"I don't know what you're talking about." She sipped her coffee. "Pretty, pretty damask."

"Shut up." He walked in the store. "We're talking about Gavin after I look at this. Don't think you've avoided the conversation."

They walked from shop to shop, with Arthur picking out a few different bolts of fabric and placing an order for a job he had the next month. Her mind circled around what Arthur had said earlier.

...your hot boss who's in love with you.

Gavin wasn't in love with her. She was human. He was a vampire. She knew it happened. After all, Beatrice had started out human—okay, *every* vampire had started out human. But Gavin wasn't settled like Ben's aunt and uncle. Beatrice and Giovanni were professor types. Gavin had clubs and bars. He relocated every few years. He moved in glamorous, powerful circles. Chloe hardly thought he was looking for a human to drag along with him.

The man could literally fly.

So what? Maybe he is *in love with you.*

Her internal voices really needed to get their shit together. One day they were telling her a relationship with Gavin was never going to work. The next day they were imagining fairy-tale endings.

Do you love him?

Nope. No, no, no, no, no. Chloe shook her head as Arthur held up a purple-and-orange print. Loving Gavin was... so damn complicated she didn't even want to think about it.

"You don't like it?" Arthur asked. "I want to make you a skirt with this. You have an orange top this exact color that would be amazing. Just a little A-line..." He shook the fabric. "Nothing?"

"Uh..." She'd been answering her internal voices, not Arthur. "I'm not really into purple lately."

"Shut up, you look amazing in purple." He put the fabric back. "Fine. Be difficult."

They shopped for another hour before Arthur found another print he insisted on buying for her. "I'm going to make you a quilted jacket and you're going to love it."

"Okay." She hooked her arm in his. "How did you know things were right with Drew?"

Arthur looked at her from the corner of his eye. "Are we finally talking about you and the sexy Scot?"

She shook his arm. "Just tell me how you knew."

He frowned. "It sounds super unromantic, but I felt very easy with him—not *that* easy—get your mind out of the gutter." He tilted his head. "Though I was that kind of easy too. But there was no drama, you know? It's the kind of relationship my parents have, to be all traditional and shit, so it feels right. We *like* each other. We have fun. He's my favorite person. I love you, but if he wasn't working today, I would have taken him shopping."

"That's so awesome."

Arthur raised a finger. "Not that things are never hard. They totally are sometimes. But the drama doesn't come from *us*, if that makes sense. The drama comes from the rest of this shitty world and we have to deal with it." He shook her arm in his. "Like a team. An amazing, sexy, impeccably dressed team."

Chloe smiled. "Yeah. I get that."

"You and Gavin work together that way. I've seen it. You *literally* work together and you do it well. That says a lot. Add all that fucking chemistry in." He purred. "I'm serious about the way that man looks at you. He looks like he wants to eat you up."

Chloe laughed. "You have no idea."

"Stop!" Arthur put his hand to his forehead and pretended to swoon. "You're killing me holding back details."

"You'll live." Chloe leaned her head on his shoulder as they walked. Arthur was only a few inches taller than she was, and he had a great shoulder. "I love you, Arthur. Thank you for not dropping me when I was a shitty friend."

"I would never."

They walked in silence for another block, making their way back to Penn Station with bags slung on their arms. "You know, I gave Paulo shit the other day, but Drew and I *are* kind of boring and I love it that way. It may not sound sexy, but I don't see you wanting a lot of friction either."

"Yeah." She sighed. "I think I've had my share for a lifetime."

He wiggled his shoulder. "Unless it's the *good* kind of friction. If you know what I mean."

She smiled. "I know what you mean."

"Yeah, I *bet* you do."

She laughed into his shoulder. "Stop."

"You wish."

Gavin woke to the sound of a clock ticking in an unfamiliar room. He opened his eyes wide. No lethargy. No torpor. He was asleep; then he was awake.

The ceiling was white and smooth. Light came from a small lamp plugged into a socket in the corner.

His lungs rose and fell in a human rhythm. The air smelled of plaster dust, burned plastic, vanilla and coconut oil.

It took him only a few moments to remember where he was. Ben and Tenzin's safe room. There had been construction recently, explaining the plaster dust and burned plastic. It was the smell of electrical wiring work. The other smells, vanilla and coconut oil, meant Chloe had washed her hair.

He could hear her on the floor above, walking back and forth in what he thought was the kitchen area. She had one of her playlists on the speakers. Gavin smiled. Was she cooking? The air smelled faintly of tomato sauce.

He glanced at the phone next to him on the bedside table. He hit a button and saw that he'd received seven voice mails, fifteen text messages, and forty-seven emails while he'd been sleeping.

Ignoring the notifications, he dialed Audra. "Anything to report?"

"Do you want an activities report?"

He hesitated, his territorial instincts battling with his sense. Did he want to know every step she'd taken that day? Yes. Was it any of his business if it didn't affect her safety? "No. Safety assessment only."

"Nothing to report. No one following her. Nothing out of the ordinary. She's at the loft. And I'm assuming you are too."

"Is Vivian at my apartment?"

"Last I checked in with Hassim."

"Good." He stood. "You're off duty until tomorrow."

"Night, boss."

"Good night."

Gavin stood and looked for something he could use for clothes. Nothing. He'd left his wet clothes on the floor above. He wrapped a towel around his waist, unlocked the intricate set of locks securing the room, and walked upstairs.

He stood at the threshold of the kitchen, watching her hips move to the music as she rinsed something in the sink. Chloe was a dancer. It had taken Gavin some time to realize she danced to *everything*. Music in the house. At the bar. She even danced a little in the elevator. Her life was lived in movement, and it was his pleasure to watch.

Imagine if you could watch her forever.

Too soon. Far, far too soon. For the moment the point was to ensure her safety while Vivian was in town.

Gavin said, "Do you intend to keep me naked while I'm here?"

She jumped and turned around, but Gavin was pleased to see a smile on her beautiful face. "Hey. And that sounds like an excellent idea if you ask me."

"Hmmm, good to know you like me naked." He walked over, gripping the towel at his waist, and wrapped his arm around her. He bent down and kissed her full on the mouth, stroking her tongue with his, letting the heat between them build until she was gasping.

Chloe's breasts pressed to his bare chest. Damp hands came to rest on his shoulders. He slid his hand down and cupped her bottom, pulling her closer as he bent her backward over the counter.

Gavin pulled away. "Give me one good reason I shouldn't put ye on this counter, strip off these clothes, and show ye how I like to wake up in the evening."

Chloe blinked. "Uh..."

He lifted her up and set her on the counter. "Didn't hear a good argument."

"I really don't have one."

Gavin dropped the towel and pulled the smooth grey leggings and her lace-trimmed panties down her glorious legs. He spread her thighs and stroked two long fingers inside her before he gripped his erection and entered her with one hard stroke.

Dear glorious fuck, it was even better than the night

before. He felt randy as a schoolboy, and all he could think was *Chloe, cock, good.*

Chloe was laughing against his chest. "I swear, no one curses like a Scotsman."

"I have no idea what I just said."

"In all honesty, neither do I, but I think I'm flattered?"

"Ye should be." He groaned. "Dammit, woman." He leaned over and kissed her senseless. "You undo me, Miss Reardon."

Her breath hitched. "Gavin."

"Yes?" He began to move slowly back and forth, running his fingers across the top of her thighs.

"Nothing." She threw her arms around his shoulders and her legs around his waist. Then she whispered in his ear, "You undo me too."

He sat at the counter in the trousers Chloe had dried for him, meticulously sorting through his emails as she finished cooking dinner. He forwarded most of the messages to Veronica. He deleted others. Answered one himself.

Chloe was making meatballs as a marinara sauce simmered on the stove and Halsey sang in the background.

Gavin glanced at the voice mails. Two from Veronica, three from Renard. One from Cormac and another from the manager at the Bat and the Barrel.

He set his phone on the counter. "Notepaper?"

"Notepaper? So old-fashioned."

"Well, in case you weren't aware of it, Miss Reardon, I am the definition of old-fashioned."

"You?" She smiled. "I hang out with people thousands of years older than you." She pointed over her shoulder. "Pencils and Post-its in the drawer by the phone."

"Thanks." He walked over, kissing her shoulder as he passed her. "Good to know I'm not too old for you."

"Well, you are. But you're too old for pretty much anyone with a regular pulse. I can't hold it against you."

"I beg to differ, dove." He ran a hand over the curve of her ass. "Hold it all against me, and I'll thank you for the pleasure."

He walked back to the kitchen while she was laughing at him. Gavin set his phone to speaker and listened to the voice mail from his manager first. The manager had a simple ordering question. Gavin texted him before he moved to the voice mail from Cormac. He didn't listen to that one on speaker.

Cormac was wondering who the fuck Renard was and why the man was calling him like they were friends. Cormac hadn't given anyone his number. How had Renard even gotten it?

Gavin pressed his eyes shut and sighed.

"Problem with the bar?"

"Problem with Vivian." He called Cormac immediately. "Sorry, old man."

"Who the fuck is this guy, and how did he get my number?"

"Vivian's day man. I did not give your number to him, and I have no idea how he got it."

"I have to change my number again." Cormac growled. "I really hate changing my number, Gavin."

"Give me half an hour. He won't bother you again."

Cormac was silent.

"Would I say it if it wasn't true?"

"Half an hour." Cormac hung up.

Chloe was pouring the marinara over the spaghetti. "This will be ready in ten minutes."

"You're a treasure. This shouldn't take long." He dialed Renard's number and walked over to the french doors, the phone to his ear.

"Hello?"

"You don't know Cormac O'Brien's phone number anymore, Renard."

The man tried to bluff. "I don't answer to you, Gavin. Vivian told me—"

"I don't give a flying fuck what Vivian told you, ya naff bampot." His voice dropped and his brogue got thicker. "Shut yer puss and put her on the phone."

Renard went silent, and Gavin heard Vivian in the background.

"Put her. On the phone."

"Vivian."

His sister's voice came over the line. "Gavin, where are you?"

"None of your business. You don't know Cormac O'Brien, Vivian."

Her voice was breezy and annoyed. "I need his whiskey casks."

"No, you *want* them." He kept his voice low and lethal. "It's not the same thing, and you're not in France, Vivian. No one here gives a shit who you fucked in 1923. No one cares who you are until I tell them to care, so shut the *fuck* up before you screw my own operation, ye ken? You don't know Cormac's numbers. You don't know his people. You don't know anyone in the state of New York unless I personally introduce you. Are we clear on this?"

Her voice was no longer breezy, but she was still annoyed. "Do you think you're better than me?"

"No, I know it."

"You arrogant bast—"

"Who's asking for favors, Vivi?"

She was silent.

"Who?"

"Do you have a point?"

His voice rose. "You don't know Cormac O'Brien. You—and definitely fucking Renard—lost his phone number. Are we clear?"

"Fine." She hung up.

Gavin let his head fall back and he groaned. "Fuck this. She shows up in the city, expects me to open doors for her, then she pulls a stunt like this? Fuck this and fuck that scabby roaster of a day man too."

Chloe said, "And here I used to be sad I was an only child."

Her wry tone of voice managed to wrest a smile from him. "Don't be. She's a pain in my arse."

"So why even take her calls?"

"Because she's the closest thing I have to family. And in our world, that does matter. She may do ma nut in, but if I ever actually needed her, she'd be loyal."

"Well, that's good, I guess."

He watched her. "You don't ever have the urge to reconcile with your parents?"

"Uh... why?" Chloe lifted the pot of pasta and took it to

the sink. "It's a one-way relationship. From what you say about Vivian, at least if you needed her, she'd be there for you. My parents really only care about themselves."

"Are you sure about that?"

She smiled sadly. "Ten months after I moved here, I called them. I'd found a roommate. Found a job. Had managed to kind of make it on my own, and I was proud of that, you know? I wasn't a smashing success, but I didn't expect that. And I thought..." She set the pot to the side and poured the pasta in a dish. "I thought if they didn't respect what I was trying to do—turn dancing into a profession—then they'd at least respect the hard work."

Gavin set his phone on the coffee table and walked to the counter. "And they didn't?"

"They kind of brushed it off with polite sounds. Then they proceeded to go on and on about all their friends' kids—the ones who had gotten into Stanford and Yale and Harvard—and how they were doing. What internships they would get when they graduated. How proud their parents were. They did not ask about auditions. They didn't ask about my ushering job. Nothing."

"They're dobbers," he muttered. "Utter dobbers."

She laughed. "Yeah. They are."

"And they don't deserve you."

Chloe sighed and shrugged. "I'm sure they would say they deserve better. But I couldn't keep being someone I wasn't. I couldn't keep following their dreams and not my own. I didn't have any illusions like they accused me of having. I just knew that I wanted what I wanted. And even if I had tons of money, I'd be miserable if I followed their path."

"Money doesn't make you happy." Gavin took the dish from her and held it while she poured the sauce over the top. "Trust me, I have plenty."

"But you're not miserable the way my parents are," Chloe said. "So what makes you happy, Gavin Wallace?"

The corner of his mouth lifted. "Besides you?"

Her cheeks flushed with pleasure. "I'm flattered."

"You should be." He set the dish on the counter and waited for her to get plates and forks. "Being good at what I do makes me happy. Being respected makes me happy."

"Being feared?"

He frowned. "Fear can be useful in my world, but it's a tool I use very sparingly. For my purposes, I can accomplish more if people trust me. Though part of that trust is a genuine fear that I'll bring hell if anyone crosses my rules. But an equal part is people knowing that unless they break my rules, I don't care who they are or what they do."

She bit her lip as she set the table. "Ben says you deal with some pretty shady people."

His territorial instincts went on alert. "Was that him warning you away from me?"

"Uh... no." She wrinkled her forehead. "I don't think so. He just wanted me to know."

"There's less of that at the Dancing Bear than at the Bat and Barrel, but he's not wrong. The point is, as long as they don't bring their problems into my place of business, then they won't come to any harm under my roof. Does that make sense?"

"Yeah. But that also means you might serve awful people—vampires—you know what I mean. They could be killers, thieves... I can't even imagine."

"You're not wrong." Gavin chose his words carefully, partly to reassure her, but partly because it was an idea that had haunted him at times. "But think of it this way: Every society needs a meeting place. A common ground, so to speak. If there's no chance of safe meeting—of neutrality—then every meeting will end in violence. Every problem will be solved with actions instead of words."

Chloe smiled. "So you're a diplomat?"

"Every barman is a diplomat, dove. Some are just better at it than others."

She put the meatballs in a bowl and set both dishes in the middle of the small dining table. "Okay, enough philosophy. Time to eat."

"We eat." He walked to the table. "And then we plan."

"We need plans?"

"Yes. I like having plans." *And I like making them with you.*

7

The plan was Chloe would stay at the loft while Vivian was in town, play host to Giovanni and Beatrice while they were there, and not overreact when Gavin told her he was having her followed.

> *"You did* what?"
>
> *"I don't need to know where you go or who you go out with, but spare me a thought, dove. If I don't know you're safe, I'll more than likely go mad."*

Having had experience with more than one territorial vampire, Chloe eventually relented. After all, Ben was *human* and he'd done the same thing. Ben didn't know that Chloe knew about the bodyguards after she left Tom, but Tenzin had told her when Chloe confessed to feeling jumpy. In the end, knowing someone was watching to make sure her ex didn't come close was reassuring, not invasive.

She figured she could put up with it again if it kept Gavin from going mental.

Gavin had left for the Bat and Barrel around ten, and it was nearly midnight when Chloe heard the knock on the door.

Yay! More territorial vampires!

She opened the door to Beatrice De Novo, Chloe's favorite librarian badass. "Beatrice, hi!"

"How are you?" She enveloped Chloe in a hard hug—sometimes she forgot her own strength. "I miss you. You and Ben need to come out and visit more."

"Or you could just keep coming to New York." Chloe stepped back, allowing what felt like a small crowd into the loft. "How many people—?"

"Just four. Don't panic. Beatrice and me, Sadia and Dema are staying here." Ben's Uncle Giovanni stepped forward and gave Chloe a slightly softer side hug since he was carrying a sleeping toddler. "The rest have found accommodations elsewhere and are just helping to deliver..." He looked slightly bewildered. "Stuff."

So much stuff. Since Beatrice and Giovanni had adopted their daughter Sadia, they moved with slightly less stealth than most vampires. Their two designer suitcases were joined by more and more kid stuff as the men with them delivered various bags in green and pink, a backpack shaped like a horse—make that a unicorn—a car seat, a high chair, and three canvas tote bags of books.

Chloe blinked. "Uh... wow."

Beatrice's smile was strained. "Giovanni likes to be prepared for all eventualities."

"Well, you... seem prepared." Luckily the loft, though

short on sleeping space, was large on room. "We can move all her toys and books down to the practice area. With Tenzin and Ben gone, I'm only in there to dance. So no weapons and lots of room for her to run around."

A trim young woman stepped forward. "If you'll show me the training area, I can double-check it for any nonapparent risks."

That had to be Dema, the bodyguard nanny. The woman's skin was a smooth light brown, and her hair was covered neatly by a light grey hijab that brought out the unusual olive green of her eyes. She moved with military precision as she surveyed the room.

"I'll show you." Giovanni handed Sadia to Beatrice. "The stairs will be the biggest concern." He looked around. "But it looks like they've already delivered the gates."

"After we've gone over the lower floor, we should start on this one," Dema said. "I can already tell there are quite a few areas that could be a potential problem."

"Agreed." Giovanni and Dema walked downstairs.

"This is quite a production," Chloe said quietly.

"If I didn't have Dema," Beatrice said, "I would go insane."

"I can only imagine. Are you working much? Or mom stuff only right now?"

Beatrice rubbed Sadia's back as the little girl snored quietly. "I've started back on a couple of projects in the past month. Simple things that don't require travel. Mostly research with Zeno and Fina. Organizing the collection. Things like that."

"Nice."

Beatrice nodded. "It's good to have some time to just be

in work. Sadia conks out between eleven and midnight most days, so after that we can both work."

So weird. So, so weird. "Do you want to put her down? Does she sleep with you guys, or...?"

"No, she'll sleep in Ben's room, I think. Dema can share with her since she'll be with her throughout the day."

"Okay, no problem. And you know all the downstairs except for my room and Ben's is light safe, right?" Chloe knew Beatrice didn't sleep normal vampire hours. She was somewhere between Gavin and Tenzin, but she didn't want to assume.

"Yep. I'll be fine. I'm gonna go lay her down. You do what you do and don't worry about us while we're here." Beatrice smiled as she started toward the stairs. "Though I hope Sadia and I can go to one of your rehearsals, if that's okay. I'd love to see you dance, and I think Sadia will be fascinated. She already dances around any time music is playing."

"Oh, that's so cool! And I'd love if you visited. Most rehearsals are after work hours, so this time of year you'd have no trouble coming. I usually split time between here and Gavin's, but he has company this week too, so I'll be around."

At the mention of Gavin, Beatrice's smile tightened. Just a little. "Cool. We'll work it out then. I'm excited."

Chloe had forgotten that Beatrice wasn't Gavin's biggest fan. According to Ben, it stemmed from something that happened when his aunt was still human, but he wasn't clear on what it was.

Not my circus, Chloe thought, *not my monkeys.*

But she couldn't lie that it bothered her just a little that two of her favorite vampires clearly didn't get along. What she could do to remedy the situation, she had no idea.

The furor of Giovanni and Beatrice's arrival quickly wound down as Dema and the two drivers sorted all the stuff and the baby was put to bed. Chloe texted Gavin before she retreated to her room.

Vampire families are weird. And wonderful.

Weird I will agree with. Wonderful is debatable.

Your sister?

The string of profanities he typed made little sense to Chloe, but she got the general gist.

I'm going to have to google most of those, she typed back.

Wise, considering that as long as Vivian is in town, you'll be hearing them.

Going to bed. Night.

Wish I was with you. See you tomorrow evening.

Gavin called Chloe into the Bat and Barrel that evening, determined to ease her into some of the more complicated parts of his life. If he was in love with her and he wanted a chance at a real relationship, she would have to know. Eventually she'd have to know it all.

What are you doing, Wallace?

He sat at the far end of the bar, second-guessing every decision he'd made with her. The silent riot in his mind lasted only as long as it took to see Chloe walk through the door of the pub, raindrops sparkling in her hair and a red tint on her cheeks from the cold.

There she is. That's why you're doing this, ya daft prick.

Gavin waited for her to walk toward him, aiming for the hallway and the break room. "Good evening, Chloe."

"Gavin." She smiled. "Hi."

He'd worn a suit that evening since he had a meeting with a liquor distributor who cared about that kind of thing. He enjoyed the way her eyes scanned him, up and down, in a more proprietary manner than she'd worn before.

Excellent. He was feeling territorial, and he quite enjoyed that he wasn't the only one.

"I need to see you in my office before you start your shift," he said, glancing at the server who was polishing glasses behind the bar. "Lettie, tell Brian to cover the bar for about fifteen more minutes, will you?"

"Sure thing, boss."

He didn't give in to his urge to kiss her until they were both in his office and the door was closed and locked.

"Mmmm." She groaned against his lips. "I missed you when you woke up tonight."

"Not more than I missed you." His hand ran down the back of her thigh. "I missed these legs. This mouth." He kissed her again, openmouthed and hungry.

"How long until your sister leaves?"

"How long until Beatrice and Giovanni leave?"

She put her arms around his shoulders while he indulged in kissing every inch of her neck. "Why do we know so many people?"

He wanted to bite her, but he was waiting. He'd never fed from anyone who made him feel the way Chloe did, and he was oddly reticent. How would it feel? Would it tie him to her even more deeply? Did he want that?

He indulged in his urge to kiss her while also covering

her with his scent. She'd be working around vampires this night. He could not control the instinct to mark her, even if she wasn't yet taking his bite.

"We'll manage this week." He straightened his tie while she tied her hair back at the nape of her neck. "And then life will return to normal. Or as normal as it can be."

"Sounds good." Her lips were swollen from his kiss, and she looked a bit rumpled.

Good.

Of course, the idiocy of calling his new lover to work in his vampire-friendly bar hit him only a few minutes after she walked behind the bar. Gavin wanted to kill every immortal who spoke to her.

Yer a bampot, Wallace.

At least Vivian wasn't here. As much as he hated to acknowledge it, his sister could read him like no other immortal on earth. A consequence of their early years together, but annoying nonetheless. If he wanted to keep his relationship with Chloe private, he could not let Vivian and Chloe be in the same location.

Even those few moments at the Dancing Bear the other night had made Vivian more curious about "that pretty curly-haired server at your bar." Gavin had distracted her, but Chloe had clearly caught Vivian's attention.

Gavin settled into a corner booth for his meeting while Chloe tended the bar with Lettie, Mathias, and a new server who'd just started that night. All three wore a discreet red button on their lapels that told vampire customers they were available for feeding. There were private rooms in the back for that sort of thing, and Gavin kept all of them monitored with both video and audio surveillance. Some vampires bristled at the intrusion, but he made no secret that his servers were professionals and not pawns.

"Mr. Gardner." He rose and greeted the human in the impeccable three-piece suit. "It's a pleasure to finally meet you. Can I get you a drink?"

The meeting held no surprises, which was a relief since Gavin was distracted. He couldn't stop checking on Chloe. Who was she talking to? She'd taken a break; had she been gone longer than normal? She received a text on her phone that made her smile. Who was texting her?

Get ahold of yourself, Wallace.

It was a complication he hadn't anticipated, and one that gave him pause. Was this normal when one become attached to a human? How was he supposed to moderate his instincts when everything felt so precarious between them?

You want a commitment from her. Gavin had resigned himself to being in love, but he had no idea if Chloe's feelings ran as deeply as his own. The uncertainty was maddening.

He was checking his accounts later that evening when an unexpected visitor walked in the bar.

Giovanni Vecchio.

The notorious fire vampire caught Gavin's eye immediately and nodded in greeting. Gavin waved him over before Giovanni could find another seat.

"Hello." He rose to greet Giovanni. "I didn't know you'd be coming in tonight."

"Cormac," Giovanni said. "I'm meeting him at one."

"You're early."

"I am." Giovanni sat in Gavin's booth and folded his hands with an air of careful nonchalance. "I thought we might have something to discuss."

Ah. Well, he knew he'd have to have the conversation eventually. Tenzin had warned him. Chloe, after all, was under Giovanni's aegis, which made him her guardian in the vampire world. Lettie stopped by the table, and Gavin ordered two scotches from his private reserve.

"Both neat," he said. "And a glass of cold water. Thank you, Lettie." Gavin angled himself to face Giovanni, unwilling to appear supplicant. "You already knew we were involved."

"I did."

The two men had been allies in the past, but Gavin would hesitate to call Giovanni a friend.

"We're more involved now," Gavin said.

"I sensed that." Giovanni didn't say he'd smelled Gavin all over the loft, but he didn't have to. His scent would have been in the secure room and all over Chloe.

"I'm not asking permission," Gavin said. "Asking permission would be an insult to her and me. She's a grown woman."

"She's a young woman."

Gavin's eyes narrowed. "She's not sheltered. And she knows her own mind."

"I know both those things." Giovanni unfolded his hands and folded them again.

Good Lord. Was the vampire... nervous? The fact that Giovanni might be as uncomfortable as Gavin was put him at ease.

"Have you ever known me to be involved with a human?" Gavin asked.

"More than for your own convenience? No."

"Well then."

Giovanni's eyebrows rose. "I see."

"Do you?"

Giovanni smiled a little. "Yes, I do. I saw months ago. Your new bar speaks for itself."

Gavin felt his collar grow tight. "The Dancing Bear is a good investment. The theater crowd—"

"You didn't build it for the theater crowd. You built it for her. Coming from you, Gavin, it's practically a love letter."

Gavin rolled his eyes. "Italians. So dramatic."

"You mean observant." Giovanni released his hands to take the glass of scotch the server brought. "Don't be so defensive. I know we've never been confidants, but if anyone knows what you're going through at the moment, it's me."

Gavin glanced at the bar. Chloe caught his eye and offered an easy smile. She loved Giovanni. He was Ben's uncle, and he'd known Chloe since she was young.

Gavin forced the words through his lips. "When did you know with Beatrice?"

"You saw me after he took her," Giovanni said. "You should know the answer to that question."

The memory was one of Gavin's few regrets in life. He'd been cornered into a meeting between Giovanni and his bastard of a vampire son, Lorenzo. Lorenzo had used Beatrice as leverage and put Giovanni into an impossible situation that forced him to let his son take the woman he cared about when she'd been a vulnerable human.

Gavin had suspected Lorenzo wouldn't risk harming Beatrice; the bastard wanted her as bait.

He'd suspected. But he hadn't known.

Putting the young woman into the hands of a vampire he knew was a killer was a decision that haunted Gavin. He hadn't known how Giovanni felt about Beatrice at the time, but he'd known soon after when the fire vampire had erupted in rage and turned the vampire world red in a quest for the woman who would eventually become his mate.

Gavin sipped his scotch, unable to ease the tight grip on his glass. "Does she still curse every time my name comes up?"

"She hasn't done that in years. She appreciates what you've done for Ben."

"Ben is a friend," Gavin said. "One of the few that I care to claim."

"I know that. So does she. And she also knows you've taken our side in fights that could have meant your end."

Gavin swallowed, and the scotch burned. "Fair is fair."

"I think you've paid your debt—"

"Have I?"

"—but make no mistake; Beatrice will take your head off if you hurt Chloe."

Gavin offered a rueful smile. "She did it to Lorenzo, so I don't doubt it."

"I'm serious, Gavin."

"So am I." His eyes rose to Giovanni's. "I want to kill the vampire she's talking to at the bar."

Giovanni glanced at the grizzled vampire with silver

hair and pox scars on his face. "Isn't he one of Cormac's crew?"

"Yes. It doesn't matter. I want to kill him. I want to kill every man she smiles at. I want to hide her in the mountains and put a dozen guards on her. I'm having her followed every time she's not with me."

Giovanni's eyes were sympathetic instead of judgmental. "Does she know?"

"I told her the other night. This particular obsession is a relatively new development since..."

"I see." Giovanni took a long breath. "As long as she knows about the surveillance, you're fine. It's when you don't tell them that they get really angry. Trust me on that one. I speak from experience."

Gavin gripped his glass tighter. "Does it get better?"

Giovanni grimaced. "Honestly? No. Yes and no. Once you make your claim public, your status and alliances should help keep others away. They already keep their distance knowing she's under my aegis and one of your employees. You're in a better position than I was. You studiously avoid having enemies."

"Enemies aren't profitable."

Giovanni's voice dropped to nearly a whisper. "But Chloe will be seen as possible leverage until she becomes a power in her own right."

Fuck me. "All this... I didn't expect it. And it's not entirely welcome, to be honest."

"I understand completely. But don't second-guess yourself for taking the chance. If it's real—if it's meant to be—you'll never regret it." Giovanni spotted Cormac a few seconds after he walked through the door. "My meeting is here." He rose and finished the scotch before he looked down at Gavin. "I trust you to guard her, Gavin. Not only her safety but her heart. You're capable of both; don't doubt yourself."

Gavin watched him walk away.

Dammit, why was Giovanni fucking Vecchio making Gavin feel like he'd just patted him on the head and said "good lad"? He swallowed the rest of his drink and turned back to his paperwork.

Chloe watched Beatrice and Sadia from the corner of her eye as she completed her last set. Beatrice was smiling, and the little girl's eyes were rapt on the twisting and turning dancers. They had been in New York for three nights, and this was the first chance they'd had to watch Chloe rehearse.

When the music went silent, Chloe followed her fellow dancers to the front of the studio to sit for notes from the director, which were thankfully minimal. Then she exchanged polite good-nights with everyone as she walked to the back of the room.

"Sorry you couldn't see from the front," Chloe said. "This space is pretty cramped. Did you enjoy it anyway?"

Sadia walked toward her and held out her arms before she spun in a circle.

Chloe was delighted. "Very good, Sadia! You want to practice with me more at home?"

To answer her, the little girl toddled over to Chloe and grabbed her fingers to tug her toward Beatrice.

"I think that's a yes." Beatrice smiled. "It was great. Really great. When is the show?"

"Three weeks."

"I may have to fly out to see it. You guys already look amazing. That was wonderful."

"Thank you." It warmed Chloe's heart to have someone she respected so much compliment her. She'd never hear anything like that from her mom. She couldn't even imagine her mom coming to a performance. "The City Dance Collective is also going to be live streaming it on the first night. So if you can't come out, you should be able to watch online."

"I'll keep that in mind." Beatrice rose and held her arms out for Sadia, who went immediately to her mother. "But I'd really love to be here if we can work it out. I'll talk to Gio when we get home."

Chloe gathered her things and walked toward the door with Beatrice and Sadia following her. The car that had brought them to the rehearsal space in Hell's Kitchen was already waiting for them.

"You need to come to rehearsal more often," Chloe said. "I could get used to service like this."

Beatrice buckled Sadia into the car seat while Chloe sat on the other side. "Doesn't Gavin have a car?"

"He does. And he'd tell Abe to cart me anywhere if I let him. It just seems silly to me."

"Hmmm." Beatrice nibbled on Sadia's fingers, causing the little girl to laugh.

"I mean..." Chloe felt oddly defensive of Gavin. "He already has someone guarding me all the time as it is. It feels wasteful to have a car following me around too. It'd attract more attention."

Beatrice's eyebrows rose. "He told you about the tail?"

"Oh yeah. Like... the day after he hired her."

"Interesting."

Beatrice didn't say more than that, but Chloe sensed approval.

"So you spotted Audra?" she asked.

"Quickly. Most humans won't. She's good."

Chloe glanced behind the car where she knew Audra's motorcycle would soon be following them. "I try to pretend she's not there."

"That's usually the best policy."

Chloe felt like the elephant in the car was sitting on her chest. "Why don't you like Gavin? Can I ask? Is it for super-secret vampire reasons?"

The corner of Beatrice's mouth turned up. "Yes, you can ask. The short answer is, I don't trust him to look out for people other than himself. I think he has good tendencies—and I can't lie, he's been a friend to Ben—but I have a hard time trusting him."

"Because of something that happened to you personally?"

"Yes."

Chloe nodded. "Okay. I mean, I can't argue with that. But I guess..."

Beatrice didn't jump in. She waited for Chloe to speak as she handed Sadia a soft-sided book.

"If you acknowledge Gavin has been a good friend to Ben—someone that he can trust—why don't you think he'll be a good friend—or more than a friend—to me?"

"Honest answer?"

"Always." Chloe braced herself.

"I trust Ben to take care of himself."

It bruised her, but Chloe could only nod. What did she expect? Beatrice knew all about her ex. She knew that Chloe had allowed herself to fall into an abusive relationship. It was hardly surprising that she didn't trust her to—

"Ben grew up with us. Grew up with vampires. He started training when he was twelve. He grew up on the streets before that. You're still new to this world and I worry. I know you're smart as hell. I know you're training with Tenzin now. But I worry. I can't help it."

"Oh." The hurt eased a little. "So you don't doubt me because...?"

"Because what?"

Her voice was small. "Because of Tom. Because of what he did to me. What I allowed to happen."

Beatrice's voice cut like a blade. "You were young and you were in love. Tom's actions are his own fault. Not yours. If anything, that experience makes me less concerned for you, not more. Experience is a hard teacher, but you've earned a level of wisdom about relationships that Ben doesn't have. I don't doubt you because of that, Chloe. Don't think that even for a minute."

She nodded. "Okay."

"Do you believe me?"

Chloe forced a smile past the lump in her throat. "I do. Mostly. I'm still processing all this. The world he lives in—the world all of you live in—it's a lot to take." Chloe blinked back tears. "I've spent too much of my life being afraid, and I can't"—she forced the words past the lump in her throat—"I can't ignore that risk because of how I feel about him."

"You're smarter than I was at your age," Beatrice said. "If you need to talk, let me know. When I say I've been there, I mean it."

8

Gavin strode into his penthouse already irritable. He'd woken that night to an empty phone. He had messages, but none of them were ones he wanted to read.

He hadn't heard from Chloe. Usually she texted him during the day, and he would wake up to one or more messages from her telling him what her plans for the night were, where she was staying, or some random amusement she'd seen or heard.

He'd met with Audra in the lobby, but as he'd instructed her, she didn't report on Chloe's movements, only that she was safe and Hassim had taken over her shift since Gavin would be occupied for most of the night.

He heard movement from the living room. Walking around the corner, he saw Vivian in a purple dressing gown studying a shirtless young man. Her head was slightly cocked and she stared as the human squirmed. Renard sat in a corner, looking at his phone.

The young man looked up when he saw Gavin in the doorway, and his eyes went wide.

"Out." Gavin pointed at the door.

Without a word, the man stood, pulled on his shirt, and walked past Gavin with a mumbled apology.

Vivian stood and turned with her hands on her hips. "That was my dinner."

"And this is my apartment." He walked to the bar and took out a bottle of blood-wine. "You can have wine or you can go to the club, but don't feed in my home. Where did he come from?"

"Renard ordered out."

Gavin glanced at Renard, who only shrugged.

"There's an app," he said.

There was an app?

"Get dressed for a meeting," Gavin said. "Business meeting. I've secured an appointment with Cormac in an hour. We need to leave in fifteen minutes, so hurry."

Vivian sauntered past him, grabbed the blood-wine, and went to her quarters without a word. Gavin knew she'd be out in sixteen minutes and not a second less. She hated being ordered around.

"Renard," Gavin said.

"Yes?"

"Start packing her things. You're not invited to this meeting, and you'll both be leaving tomorrow night."

Renard looked skeptical, but he also rose and left the room.

Gavin tried not to grind his teeth. He glanced at his phone. Still nothing. He slid it back in his pocket and tried to focus.

He would get Vivian out of his hair.

Life would return to normal.

But with more Chloe.

He was determined that she needed to move in. Ben and Tenzin's loft was secure, but his apartment was just as secure, more luxurious, and he had an entire practice area for her use. She could use the car during the day if she needed it. She would sleep in one place every night instead of moving back and forth, and Gavin wouldn't have to wake up every night wondering where she was.

All he had to do was convince Cormac to sell Vivian some damn bourbon casks and hustle her back to France to play with her vineyards and rotating harem of pretty young men.

Gavin decided she'd pay for the favor in Loire Valley red. He'd heard rave reviews of her last release, and he wanted some for his cellar. Vivian annoyed the hell out of him, but he had to admit she was an extraordinary winemaker.

She exited her room in an impeccable grey suit and heels exactly sixteen minutes after she entered. Gavin chose to remain silent and escorted her to the car.

"Renard isn't—?"

"Renard isn't coming." Gavin opened the car door. "He's packing your things because you're leaving tomorrow."

Her smile was smug as she slid into the black sedan. "So you've convinced him?"

"No, you're going to convince him." Gavin closed the door, walked around to the driver's side, and gave Abraham instructions before he got in the car. "I secured you a meeting, Vivi. If you can't convince him, there's no reason to stay. So you're leaving tomorrow."

She pouted, but she didn't say anything more. They arrived at Cormac's business office in twenty minutes and sat in a comfortable reception area while his personal secretary announced their arrival.

Cormac arrived only moments later. The vampire didn't bother with some of the mind games others of their kind enjoyed. He was blunt, and Gavin appreciated that about him.

Vivian got straight to the point after obligatory introductions. "I want to buy twenty of your bourbon casks."

"Why?"

She frowned. "Why?"

"Yeah." Cormac leaned back in his chair. "Why?"

His office was as eccentric as he was. The desk was an antique, but the chair behind it was a battered wooden thing with cracked vinyl on the headrest. The shelves behind him were filled with books—actual books and not show books—as varied in subject as they were mismatched in appearance.

Agricultural journals and an outdated edition of the *Encyclopædia Britannica*. Novels in six different languages that Gavin had spotted. Motorcycle-repair books and a truly impressive collection of manga, along with a well-worn set of the Harry Potter hardbacks, original covers.

Gavin used to think that Cormac's eccentricities were for show, to throw immortals off. He'd thought Cormac was playing a clever game of disrupting expectations.

He'd come to realize that Cormac was just strange. He was a strange man with offbeat interests and little care what anyone thought of him other than his surviving brothers and his favorite child.

Vivian clearly didn't know what to think of the man. "My distiller is experimenting with brandies at the moment, and he has requested—"

"Yeah, I get that, but why do you want *my* bourbon casks?"

Vivian did not take well to being interrupted. Her tone was acid. "I'm afraid I don't understand your confusion, Mr. O'Brien. Do you have casks to sell or do you not? It's not really any of your business what I do with them."

"No, it's not." Cormac rocked forward. "I'm being nosy because I can be. Because I know that your distiller originally asked for whiskey casks, not bourbon in particular. In fact, you've been trying to buy whiskey casks for about six months now with no luck." Cormac glanced at Gavin. "So I wondered: Why won't anyone in Ireland or Scotland sell casks to Vivian Lebeau? She's not known for being cheap. She pays her bills on time. So what could it be?"

Gavin knew she had an ulterior motive. He just knew it. He forced himself not to sigh. He turned to Vivian and waited to see how she would respond.

She remained silent for a long time. "Do you have casks to sell or not?"

Cormac took his wire-rimmed glasses off and cleaned them with the edge of his shirt. "Tell Gavin why you're coming to me, and we can negotiate."

Vivian pursed her lips, but she turned to Gavin. "Because I stole the Ramsays' winemaker and they told all the whiskey makers in Britain not to return my calls."

This was the first Gavin had heard of it, but he wasn't

surprised. He owned a distillery in Scotland, but Vivian didn't know that, and the day-to-day operations were placed in the hands of a trusted manager who wouldn't bother calling him about a sales matter.

Gavin rubbed his temple. "You *stole* their winemaker, Vivian? How? And why?"

Terrance Ramsay and Gemma Melcombe were the vampire lords of London and also the immortal world's most successful blood-winemakers. But as far as Gavin knew, Vivi hadn't gotten into blood-wine. At all. She liked her wine and her blood. She did not like to mix them and only drank blood-wine if preserved blood was the only other option.

Please tell me it was money. Please tell me you offered him an insane amount of money to change wineries because of a new business opportunity you just couldn't pass—

"The man is a red-blooded one." Vivian's smile turned seductive. "And far more virile than I expected for his age. We met at an event and he was enchanted by me. What could I do?"

Gavin looked at Cormac and his eyes said it all.

Siblings.

"So you seduced the Ramsays' winemaker and convinced him to come work for you," Gavin said. "And... are you two making blood-wine now?"

Industrial espionage was hardly unknown in their world. In fact, it was considered a perfectly legitimate way to beat competitors. Gavin knew it was something else.

"No." She curled her lip. "Disgusting. Rene is taking a holiday. Deciding what he would like to pursue in the future. He's a very gifted painter, you know."

So you fucked with the Ramsays just to fuck with them and get laid.

Classic Vivian.

Gavin asked, "Cormac, how much for the casks?"

Cormac quoted a number that was at least three times the normal asking price for used bourbon casks.

Vivian began cursing him in French. Cormac looked at her, completely unperturbed.

"That's the price," he said. "I don't have to sell you anything. They're already spoken for, so I'm doing you a favor."

Vivian stood and walked out of the office, still muttering curses.

Cormac turned to Gavin. "Was that a yes?"

"Yes." Gavin stood and held out his hand. "Thank you."

"No problem." He shook Gavin's hand and held. "I hope I didn't overstep."

"You didn't. She would have told me eventually when she wanted my help to fix it."

Cormac let his hand drop. "And will you?"

Normally Gavin would. Gavin always did manage to fix Vivian's messes when she made them. But this time...

"You know," Cormac said, "sometimes with family, a little tough love is in order."

"Tough love?"

"Ramsay won't hurt her. He's got other winemakers in his operation now, so Rene wasn't a unicorn. He's annoyed with her and making a point. Fuck with me and I'll fuck with you." Cormac shrugged. "Just my take."

"Thank you for the meeting," Gavin said. "I'll make

sure Renard has your office manager's number before they leave."

"Sounds good."

Gavin walked out of the office and said polite goodbyes before he joined Vivian in the car.

Vivian angled herself toward him. "Gavin—"

"Don't." He leaned forward. "Abe, take me to the Bat and Barrel. After you've dropped me off, take Vivian back to the apartment."

"Got it, boss."

Gavin sat back in the seat and straightened his cuffs. "I'll get Renard the proper information to contact O'Brien's office for the casks."

"Aren't you going to ask me about Rene?"

"No." He came to a snap decision that was a long time coming. "I'm not helping you smooth this over with Ramsay, Vivi."

Her eyes watered dramatically. "You don't care."

"Send the human back to London with a kiss and a few cases of red. In a couple of years, Ramsay will forget this ever happened."

"But you're friendly with him. Can't you just—?"

"No." Once made, the decision was surprisingly easy to stick with, even with her dramatics. "Fix it yourself, Vivian. You don't need my help for this."

"You don't care about me." Her voice turned bitter. "You don't care about your own sister. Your *only* family."

"I do care, Vivian, but let's be honest, you only visit when you want something, you enjoy disrupting people's lives to amuse yourself, and you lie constantly."

"You lie too."

Gavin raised his eyebrows. "Do I?"

"You're enamored with that little human, and you didn't even tell me. You think I haven't heard the rumors at your bar? You think I can't tell when something has changed?"

Frost settled in his veins, and Gavin turned to his sister, all familial affection forgotten. "Forget it, Vivian. Forget her."

The corner of her mouth turned up. "Or what? Is a human more important than me? Are you going to—?"

In the space of a blink, Gavin put a hand on her throat and squeezed, just enough to make her eyes go wide. "Forget. Chloe."

Vivian's mouth dropped open.

"You don't know her. You don't use her. You don't tell anyone she's mine." Gavin dropped his hand.

Vivian rubbed her throat. "People are going to know eventually if you're acting so foolishly."

"Foolishly?" Gavin smiled. "That woman is under Giovanni Vecchio's personal aegis. She's friends with his nephew and works for Tenzin. You think I'm the only one protecting her?" The realization settled in his bones and released the knot of tension that had taken residence around his heart. "Forget her connection to me, Vivian. If you try to fuck with Chloe Reardon, you will bring down the wrath of God and Tenzin. Leave her alone. Leave us alone. Trust me when I tell you it's not worth the trouble."

His sister crossed her arms over her chest and stared out the window. She didn't speak. She didn't antagonize him. She was completely and utterly silent.

It was glorious.

~

He was sitting at his normal booth at the Bat and Barrel, still glancing at his phone. She had rehearsal tonight, then she was working her shift at the Dancing Bear. He could go there and see her. Since Vivian looked to be on the way out, it was tempting.

Why hadn't she texted him?

He felt Beatrice approaching before he saw her. Beatrice De Novo had a strong presence she took no pains to hide. He'd met her when she was still a student in Giovanni's employ, but the fact that she'd become a powerful immortal didn't surprise him. She'd had a backbone of steel even when she was human.

"Hey there." The slight Texas drawl still popped out occasionally. "Don't flinch."

"I don't make a habit of it." He waved Lettie over. "Scotch?"

"I hear that bottle Giovanni gave me came from your own distillery."

"Did you like it?" He'd given it to Giovanni so Beatrice wouldn't throw it away.

"It's tasty."

"Good. Lettie, two glasses from my bottle, please."

Lettie smiled. "You got it."

She walked away, and Gavin shuffled the paperwork he'd been pretending to read back into the file he needed to review. "What brings you to the Bat and Barrel?" he asked. "It's late."

"I have a toddler," she said. "Needed to put her to bed."

Gavin shook his head. "That is a very odd mental image."

"Try Giovanni changing a diaper." Beatrice cracked a smile. "I never thought I'd see the day."

"You and me both." Gavin waited for Lettie to set the glasses down and leave them. "Why are you here?"

Beatrice picked up her glass, sipped it, put it back on the table. "That's even better than what I remember. I hate you a little."

"Beatrice, why—?"

"You're in love with her, aren't you?"

Gavin wanted to say "none of your business," except it wouldn't be true. Chloe was their business because she was their family. And since Chloe didn't have parents in her life, he was grateful she had them.

He drummed his fingers on his glass. "Yes."

"Does she know?"

"I feel like I've been wearing my feelings like neon lights on my fucking sleeve, but that's me." He looked away. "I don't know if she knows."

"Since you're not exactly the touchy-feely emotional type, I'm going to guess she might not. And I'm going to give you some advice you need to take. You might want to ignore me out of spite. God knows I've needled you over the years, but this isn't about us. It's about her. I've been where she is, and I'm not going to bullshit you."

Gavin swallowed a sharp retort and forced himself to listen. "What is your advice?"

"Right now, imagination is her worst enemy. She'd trying to imagine what you want from her. What your feelings are. What a relationship with a vampire is going to look like. She's had relationships with humans, good and bad, but she's never had one with an immortal."

Gavin nodded. "I'm listening."

Beatrice continued. "You need to make it clear what you want from her. I'm not making any judgments or assumptions. Your relationship is between the two of you. But don't let her imagination run the show. Just tell her."

"That... is excellent advice." Between his earlier realization about Chloe's safety and Beatrice's words of experience, he felt a new sense of resolve. "Thank you, Beatrice."

"You're welcome." She sipped her drink. "I still have reservations. But I'd love for you to prove me wrong."

"Noted." He set down his glass. "For the record, he was a fucking bampot for leaving you for five years. I told him so at the time, but he never listens."

"A fucking bampot?" Beatrice smiled. "I'm going to remember that one, because... yeah. He totally was."

Chloe was cleaning up the bar when he walked in. Her heart jumped in her chest.

"Hey," she said.

Gavin walked over, ignoring Rafael who was wiping down tables and putting chairs up.

He stopped in front of Chloe, and his expression was completely unreadable. "Hello. I need to see you in the office when you're done."

Shit.

Rafael was staring at both of them with wide, concerned

eyes. Gavin walked down the hall and disappeared while Chloe finished wiping down the bar.

Shit.

Chloe felt small inside. She'd been excited when he first walked in, despite the awful mental gymnastics she'd been going through the past two days. Two days without seeing Gavin had felt like an eternity, which had made her pause.

Just how fast was she jumping into this? Sleep with a vampire one night and get addicted the next? What was she doing? Beatrice had called her smart, but she didn't feel smart. She felt lovesick.

And that scared her to death.

Chloe decided she needed to get perspective. She couldn't just jump into this headfirst. Not after the disaster that was Tom. She'd spent the day thinking about Gavin, all the while trying to distract herself from missing him. She hadn't called him. She hadn't texted. She'd thrown herself into work and spent extra time at practice. She'd had dinner with Arthur and Drew before she went to rehearsal.

And no matter what she did, her thoughts kept circling back to Gavin.

Rafael walked over to the bar. "You guys okay? Boss looked... I don't know how he looked."

She smiled big. "He's fine. He probably just..." She forced herself to stop. Making excuses for Tom's moods had been one of the first slopes she'd slid down. "Actually, I have no idea what's up. Your guess is as good as mine, Raf."

"You want me to stay?"

"No. I'll be fine." She didn't know what was going on with Gavin, but she knew that down to her bones. Whatever mood he was in, it wouldn't erupt into violence. Anything else, she could handle.

"Go ahead." He nodded toward the hallway. "I can finish this up."

"Thanks." She tossed the towel she'd been using in the cleaning bucket and washed her hands in the sink. Then she hung up her apron and walked down the hall to the small office Gavin used when he was working at the Dancing Bear. The door was cracked open.

He wasn't behind the desk but sitting on the couch opposite the doorway. It was burgundy-red crushed velvet and looked like it was made in the Roaring Twenties. Chloe had picked it out when she helped him decorate the bar. Gavin's arms were behind his head, and his feet were resting on the leather ottoman.

She'd fallen asleep on that couch while he was playing with her hair after work. They'd made out on that couch. They'd shared meals there.

Please don't dump me on my favorite couch.

"Hey."

He smiled a little and patted the space next to him. "Hey, yourself."

Chloe walked over and sat next to him. "Everything all right?"

"Should I ask you the same?" He turned his head. "You didn't text today."

She tucked her hair behind her ear. "I got busy with work, and then I went over to Arthur's for dinner. The night kind of got—"

"You don't need to explain yourself," he said. "You're not required to check..." He frowned. "No, I shouldn't lie. It bothered me. More than I'd expected. I enjoy seeing those little messages from you when I wake up. They always make me smile, and since you're usually the only one who texts me without stating a problem I need to fix, I've come to count on them to start my night."

Chloe felt even smaller. "I'm sorry." He'd been honest, so she needed to be honest right back. "I was trying to prove something to myself."

He frowned. "What?"

"That I wasn't getting too attached to you days after we slept together. That I wasn't becoming some obsessed little—"

"Chloe, you've been texting me nightly for over nine months now. It has nothing to do with the two of us becoming lovers."

She put her head in her hands. "I just... I don't know what I was thinking. I've been all over the place the past few days."

"Because we made love?" He pulled her hands away from her face.

"No. Yes. Because of that and because... I don't know. Everything."

"Hmmm."

What was it with vampires and their vague nonverbal communication?

"I'm sorry I didn't text you tonight," she said. "I wanted to."

"Beatrice came and spoke to me tonight."

Her head popped up. "She did?"

"She did, and we had an actual conversation. I'm quite proud of us both."

Chloe smiled.

"There it is." He touched her cheek. "I needed to see that smile. Beatrice told me something else. She said that right now imagination is your worst enemy."

Chloe didn't know what to say. "I don't know—"

"Yes, I thought that might be the problem." Gavin sat forward on the couch, his elbows braced on his knees. "Forgive my interrupting, but I realized tonight that you *don't* know. I don't think you do, and you should."

"I should know what?"

He stared straight ahead. "You should know that I'm in love with you."

Chloe's breath fled her lungs. There was no more air in the room. None.

"I'm in love with you, Chloe Reardon." He kept his voice low and steady. "It's the first time it's happened for me since I became immortal, so you should know that you have quite a lot of power over me at the moment. And I want things from you. Many things." He turned his face to her, and the expression in his eyes was searing. "I want an exclusive and permanent relationship with you. I want you to move into my home—not this halfway arrangement we've been playing with for the past year. Move in."

Chloe's mouth was hanging open, but she couldn't speak.

"I want to bite you. I won't be able to stop drinking fresh blood from others—I'm not that old—but if you want me to refrain from taking it at the vein, I am willing to do that. In fact, I think after I drink from your vein, I might prefer not to drink from any others." His eyes fell to her thighs and his accent grew thick. "Yer not the only one with an imagination, dove."

Not enough air. Still couldn't speak.

"I realized earlier tonight that I don't need to be obsessed with someone damaging you. I'm not the only immortal who loves you. Giovanni and Beatrice do. Tenzin does. You're already known. My claim on you—should you decide to accept it—makes little difference for your safety in my world. Though don't mistake me, I do not intend to fire Audra. You still need security."

She managed to take a breath. "Gavin—"

"I love you, and I want you," he said roughly. "I want you in my world, in my bed, in my own flesh, Chloe Reardon. But I don't want you to decide anything tonight, because it's important." He grabbed her hand and pressed a kiss to her knuckles. "Abe is waiting for you. It's late. Please let him take you home. I'll find my own way back to the apartment."

Gavin rose and walked to the door, leaving Chloe stunned and speechless on the couch. She didn't know what to think past the fact that Gavin loved her. *Loved* her. Everything he wanted? She didn't know where to start.

"Oh." He turned at the door. "And my sister is leaving tomorrow. She'll be out of the penthouse by ten."

"Okay." Her voice sounded tiny. "Gavin, I—"

"Please." His eyes pleaded with her. "Give me a day. At least think about everything I've said for twenty-four hours. I know I'm asking for a lot, but give me a day."

And without another word, he walked out the door.

9

Gavin woke the next night to twenty-eight messages—two of them from Chloe—six voice mails, and thirty-seven emails.

The texts from Chloe were the only ones that made him smile.

Did you know a rat can carry a chicken drumstick? They can. I may never eat chicken again.

A picture of a rat with said drumstick in his mouth looked like it had been taken in the subway and had been sent at two forty-five in the afternoon.

Just kidding, I love fried chicken. No hate for the rat.

Nothing could stop his smile.

There was nothing else. No returned affection. No gleeful "Yes, I'll move in!"

Ye told her to take twenty-four hours, ya fucking dobber.

But Chloe had heard that he missed her texts and she'd sent him something to make him smile.

She loves you.

You're not that lucky.

But maybe...

He could hear Renard speaking with Veronica in the living area outside. The automatic locks that secured his day chamber clicked open at sunset, but no one in the household would bother him until he emerged.

He tapped Audra's number on his phone. "Report?"

"Nothing much. Giovanni Vecchio left the city last night. Beatrice and her family are still in the house. No apparent threats. Their daughter's bodyguard spotted me but didn't approach."

"Good. Put Hassim on night detail. I'll let him know if he can clock off."

"You got it, boss. Have a good night."

"Thank you, Audra."

Gavin rose from bed and looked around his starkly masculine room. It was luxurious in a simple way. His were the only tastes that mattered here. Deep browns and light greys gave the room a warm, organic feeling. The bed and dresser were made of mahogany. The bed linens were rich, but decoration was sparse.

What would Chloe think of it? He'd never brought a human lover into this room, but he liked the idea of Chloe leaving her scent in it. Enjoyed the thought of modifying things to please her.

Instead of paintings, frosted false windows had been built into the room, lit to give the feeling of sunrise and sunset but without any actual danger. Gavin had learned long ago that he needed a sense of time to remain sane, even as an immortal. The few times he woke during the day, he needed the suggestion of light. In the past, he used a lamp or built his houses to allow indirect light. Technology made life for the modern vampire a bit easier.

The television in the corner turned on automatically at sunset, playing a program on the nature channel that recorded sunrises and sunsets in far-flung locations. Tonight it was a sunset in Ibiza. The midnight blue of the sky echoed the glimmering water.

Would Chloe like Ibiza? He had a club there he'd started in the sixties. Maybe it was due for a spot check.

If she wanted to come with him. If he hadn't scared her off.

Gavin walked to the shower and turned on the water, trying not to second-guess himself. The conversation had been necessary. There was no use wasting their time or playing around the edges of a relationship if it wasn't what both of them wanted. He was no longer interested in taking a casual lover.

He ignored the vulnerable feeling of throwing his heart into Chloe's lap to see what she'd do with it. She was a kind person. If she didn't want what he did, she wouldn't be cruel. Polite rejection might crush his heart, but he'd lived without it beating for a century. He'd survive. He always survived.

Whether he'd be able to step away from her was another question.

Gavin finished washing up and chose his uniform for the night, a worn T-shirt and a comfortable pair of old jeans. He didn't have any meetings tonight, and he wasn't planning to go anywhere. He'd get Vivian out of the house and then wait.

Because he was a fucking idiot.

He walked out of his room and saw Vivian's luggage piled in the entryway. Veronica was checking something on a clipboard—she did love her clipboards—and Renard was acting as Vivian's mule, carting things out of the bedroom.

Gavin went to find his sister. Vivian was standing at the vanity in the guest room, staring at her face.

"Vivi?"

"Can you see it, Gavin?"

He walked over, tilted her chin to the side, and answered the same way he had for a century. "Not even a little bit."

The burn that their sire had once left on her was so deep it had taken a decade to heal. Vivian had been young when the bastard had done it. She'd been annoying him one night, so he purposely dragged her out of her light-safe room and laid her in a place the sunrise would touch her.

She woke long before the damage could kill her, but the scar had remained for a long time.

"Are you going to make things right with Ramsay?" He straightened the coat she'd thrown over her shoulders.

"Probably." She shrugged. "Rene is boring me. And his paintings aren't as good as he thinks." Vivian turned, brushed a kiss across Gavin's cheek, and walked out of the room. "*Au revoir, mon loup.* I will see you next time."

He stayed in the guest room for a few more minutes, listening to his sister take her leave. He heard Veronica exchange goodbyes with Renard, heard the both of them discussing travel details and car services.

The front door closed and the apartment went silent.

Gavin walked to Chloe's room and pushed the door open. Her scent surrounded him.

God, he'd been a fool thinking that he could hide her from his sister. He'd been annoyed that she hadn't moved in, but her presence was everywhere. Hair things on the bedside table. A spare charger by the dresser. A jacket she'd left draped on a chair.

Gavin swallowed hard and forced his fangs back in his jaw.

She would do what she would do. The ball was in her court, as Benjamin would say.

Gavin heard a knock on the front door and wondered if Veronica had forgotten something. Despite her years working for him, she still knocked if she knew he was home.

"Veronica, you just walked out, you really don't—" It wasn't Veronica. It was Chloe.

"Hi." She looked nervous. "I didn't need twenty-four hours."

BUTTERFLIES WERE a riot in her belly. He looked so good. His hair was a little damp, and he smelled like soap and leather. She stepped into the apartment when he didn't move. "I didn't want to use my key when you weren't expecting me."

"Chloe—"

"Nope." She held up a hand. "My turn to talk. You said a lot last night." She sat on the couch and folded her hands in her lap. Then she stood again. She couldn't think when she was still. "You said a lot, and I didn't say anything back, and I apologize for that, but I was really shocked, okay?"

She walked through the living room and into the practice room, kicking off her shoes.

Gavin followed her. "I understand."

Chloe paced back and forth because she had the absurd desire to run through ballet positions, and the wood beneath her feet steadied her. "You said all that and then you left, which... I'm sorry, that wasn't cool."

Gavin smiled. "I wanted to give you time to think."

She spun around. "But I think so much! I think so damn much, Gavin. I *over*think things, okay? Look what happened when Vivian first came. I jumped to conclusions based on almost nothing because I was so afraid. Because her showing up was like every bad fantasy I'd ever had of what it would be like to fall in love with you, only to have you realize that I wasn't really all that special. That I wasn't exciting or brave or adventurous enough for you."

"Chloe—"

"Nope." She held up a hand again and kept pacing. "I told you, it's my turn."

Gavin took his boots off and sat cross-legged in the corner of the practice room. "I'm listening."

His steady attention and fixed eyes calmed her down. "I'm not brave. Not like Tenzin. Not like Ben."

"I'm not in love with them."

"I don't want grand adventures any more exciting than climbing Machu Picchu or learning how to scuba dive. That is my idea of adventure. And I do want to do both of those things."

He nodded. "Noted."

"I'm not looking to go off on treasure hunts. Or find lost libraries. Or... anything like that."

Gavin smiled. "Chloe, I know."

She nodded and stared at him. "Okay. I was just making sure."

His eyes were everything she wanted to see. Tender and warm and steady. They looked at her like...

That's what love looks like, Chloe.

She came and knelt in front of him. "I fell in love with Tom so fast I lost my head. I tumbled and fell and when things went bad, love felt like a weakness. But you don't make me feel weak. Nothing about being with you makes me feel less. I feel more. You make me feel brave. Maybe not finding buried treasure brave, but every day and every night brave."

He reached up and tucked a curl behind her ear. "Moving into my apartment brave?"

The words caught in her throat, and all she could do was nod.

Gavin drew her into his lap. "Loving me brave?"

"Yes." Tears came to her eyes. "I love you. I love you so much, and I—"

He captured her mouth before she could say more. Gavin gripped her nape and wrapped his arm around the small of her back, plastering Chloe to his chest so hard that she could feel his heart thump against her breast.

"I love you." He released her mouth. "I love you so damn much."

"I love you too."

She kissed him, running her fingers through his hair as she brought his mouth to hers. She straddled his lap, bracing herself over him, and felt Gavin's hands run down her back and over her ass. He released her nape and gripped her bottom with both hands.

"Fuck me, I love this ass." He nipped her neck. "Love these thighs." He picked her up and set her on her back as he braced himself over her, kicking her legs out so he could settle between. "Love everything about you, but I fucking love your thighs."

Gavin left her on her back and sat up, hooking his fingers in the waistband of her pants as he offered her a wicked grin. "May I, dove?"

"Yes." She shimmied out of her pants as he stripped them off and tossed them over her shoulder. "I'm going to move in."

"Good." He was staring at her legs, running his fingers up and down.

"You said an exclusive and permanent relationship?"

"Yes."

"Agreed. Though we're going to have to wait on just how permanent, if you know what I mean. That's a big decision, and I'm definitely not there yet."

He locked eyes with her. "Understood."

Gavin bent over and lifted her knee up. He kissed the inside, laving his tongue up her thigh.

Chloe forced the words through lips that only wanted to moan. "And I want you to bite me."

Gavin froze. "Say that again?"

"I want you to bite me. I've been wanting you to bite me for months. Yes, it makes me question my sanity a little, but I'm just going with it. Bite me and drink from me."

He let her leg drop and moved up her body. He pressed his lips to hers in a whisper-soft kiss. "Are you sure?"

She nodded. “It doesn’t hurt, right?”

“Not even a little.” The corner of his mouth turned up. “Maybe a bit if you want it. Like a love bite. I’d quite like you to turn your teeth on me.”

“Really?”

“Oh yes.” He reached down and teased the soft flesh between her thighs. “Where do you want me to bite you?”

Her cheeks flushed. “Down there.”

His fingers teased the inside of her thigh. “Here?”

Chloe’s pulse was a stampede. She nodded.

“Are you sure?”

“Yes. But take your clothes off.”

Gavin stood quickly and stripped off his shirt and unbuckled his pants. “This is why kilts are superior to all other clothes.”

“Easy access?”

He shoved his jeans and boxers down. “Exactly.”

Chloe’s mouth went dry. “Hi, there.”

Gavin smiled and looked around the wooden floor of the practice room. “Here?”

“I’m not picky.”

Gavin knelt down and scooped her up. “I am.”

Chloe didn’t like to be carted around by anyone who wasn’t a professional, but she supposed Gavin had privileges. He carried her out of the practice room and down the hall to his own chamber. Then he tossed her on a rumpled bed.

She looked around. “This is your room.”

“Yes.” He crawled on top of her and teased apart the buttons on her blouse. “It is.”

“You let me in your room.”

"Yes." His face turned serious. "I let you into my heart, Chloe Reardon. A bedroom is hardly that extraordinary."

The warmth in her chest was something she'd never experienced before. A settled, sure rightness.

I am going to love you forever.

"You're a good man," she whispered.

"I'm good for you." He stroked his hands down her body and knelt between her legs. "And you are so very good for me."

Chloe had expected the warm kisses and laving tongue. She couldn't keep her eyes off him. The sight of his head between her legs was enough to make her see stars. What she wasn't expecting was the hot, buzzing sensation that crept under her skin, making her feel light-headed as he kissed higher.

"Is that amnis?" She gasped when his tongue found her center.

"A little. Do you like it?"

"Fuck yes." She couldn't keep her eyes on him. They rolled back in pleasure as he wound her up. The mounting pleasure grew and grew until she felt his mouth on her thigh. Felt his teeth grow long as he pressed them to her skin. "*Yes.*"

The pleasure cascaded as his fangs pierced her skin. He pulled from her vein and stroked her clitoris as her back arched in the most powerful orgasm she'd ever experienced. Shivers ran over her body. Her skin felt ultrasensitive. Every inch of her came alive under his hands and mouth and body.

Gavin pulled hard on her thigh, then she felt his tongue swipe over her skin. He rose over her and entered her when the climax was still giving her aftershocks. His lips were swollen and his skin was flushed.

Because of me.

Chloe pulled his mouth to hers and tasted the edge of iron in his kiss. He lifted her knee with his hand and entered her at a deeper angle. She hooked her leg around his waist and pulled him closer.

Closer.

Never close enough.

"My love." Gavin gasped against her neck, scraping his teeth along her skin, but he didn't bite. "My sweet, sweet love."

He muttered curses when he came.

Chloe didn't understand a single one.

GAVIN HELD her as she slept. She was lying in his bed. His scent covered her skin. Her blood flowed in his body.

The sigh he gave was of deep, deep contentment.

Chloe's curls tickled his nose, but he didn't move. She was sleeping with her head in the curve of his shoulder and her arms wrapped around his waist. Their naked legs were tangled together.

He would not have moved for all the whiskey in the world.

She slept for a half an hour, murmuring under her breath, and woke with languid eyes and a long stretch.

Chloe looked up and smiled. "Hi."

"Hello." Gavin met her smile with his own. "Did you have a nice nap?"

"I did. This bed is really comfortable." She looked around the room. "I always wondered what your room looked like."

"Just this. Not very exciting. Though you improve it."

She smiled, then abruptly narrowed her eyes. "You're not going to want me to..."

"Sleep in here all day with me? Party all night?" He smiled. "No, dove. You're welcome to wake me up in the evening if you're home, but it'd be a bit maddening for you to be locked in all day. You have a life."

"Okay. Good. That was one thing I wasn't sure of."

"Also, I look a bit dead when I'm sleeping. No need for you to see that."

She wrinkled her nose. "Dead?"

"Cold. No breath. It's not attractive."

She shuddered. "I'm sure I'll get used to the idea eventually, but right now I can't imagine." She snuggled against him. "I hope you don't have to go anywhere tonight."

He shook his head. "I took the night off."

"Nice. I switched shifts with someone at work without telling my boss. I hope he doesn't fire me."

A laugh rumbled in his chest. "Me too. I've heard you talking about him. Sounds like a right dobber."

She looked up with laughing eyes. "He's not so bad."

"Let's hope not."

"I packed three boxes today. Abe will have to help me move them. And most of my clothes are packed in my suitcases. I borrowed a couple of Ben's too."

Satisfaction. Warmth. *Victory.*

He'd keep quiet about the sense of victory. "I can also

help. I'm quite handy at carting around objects as long as I have access to roofs."

Her eyes went wide. "You are, aren't you?"

"You just realized I could take you flying, didn't you?"

Chloe's cheeks flushed. "Ahhh, yeah? But I'm not sure I want to."

He pinched her bottom. "We'll work up to that."

"Do you have a harness... or something? Like one of those skydiving things they use for tandem jumps?"

Gavin burst into laughter. "D'ye think I'm going to drop ye, lass?"

"I don't know!" She slapped his shoulder. "Maybe?"

He pulled her mouth to his. "I'd never. Never ever."

"Okay. Just put it down to my own nerves, okay? I told you I wasn't adventurous."

His heart gave a soft, quiet thump. "Just adventurous enough to love me."

She crossed her arms over his chest and set her chin on them. "You're not a risk, Gavin. I'd say you're a solid investment."

He twisted a curl around his finger. "Love you, dove. More than I can even tell you."

"It's nice to be told." She reached for his hand and knit their fingers together. "It's even nicer to be shown."

"D'ye love me, Chloe Reardon? I'll never get tired of hearing it."

"I love you, Gavin Wallace. Let me show you how much."

EPILOGUE

Gavin looked up from the trade magazine he was reading. "What's that sigh?"

"Oh nothing." Chloe shook her head and set her tablet down. "Nothing really. I have to stop opening these emails."

They were sitting in the apartment, and a dance competition show was on television, but Chloe was checking her email during the commercial break.

"What emails?"

"This animal shelter. I worked over there for about six months a few years ago and got added to the email list. Now they send one out every time they're running out of room and animals need to get adopted. They have these profiles... They're cute, but it's not practical."

"Which one are you looking at?" He reached for her tablet only to see it flicker. Chloe didn't have a reinforced case he could touch. "Ah, never mind. Don't want to break your device."

"This one." She held up her tablet and turned it back

on. The image of a sleek black cat appeared. "'Pete is a neutered male, two years young, looking for his forever home. An American shorthair that likes his humans affectionate and his whiskey neat. He's a well-traveled former rogue who likes heights and being scratched behind the ears.'"

"Fucking hell," Gavin muttered. "It's me in cat form. Do you think he really likes whiskey?"

She giggled. "No, they just add in all these things to make people keep reading. They're like silly dating profiles. Only for animals."

"Oh, I don't know." Gavin leaned over and looked at the cat again. "His name's Pete? He looks like he wouldn't pass up a finger of scotch if you offered."

Chloe set the tablet down. " He's cute, but like I said, it's not very practical."

Gavin frowned. "Why not?"

She turned to him. "What?"

"Why isn't a cat practical? They're low-maintenance animals. Neat. Friendly to apartments." He glanced around at his leather furniture and bit his tongue. "If you want a cat, get a cat."

Her eyes were wide. "You wouldn't mind?"

"Chloe, it's your house too." He tugged on a lock of her hair. "I appreciate you not bringing one home without telling me, but if you want a cat, there's no reason not to get one. When we're gone, Veronica can watch him. She's here most nights anyway."

They would be traveling. Gavin had already bought her tickets to Ibiza, he just hadn't shown them to her yet.

"Are you serious?" Her voice was pitched at least an

octave up.

"I'm serious." He smiled. "Get two if you want. Though Pete looks like a one-woman cat, if you ask me. He might not want to share you."

"Gavin, you're the best."

He smiled and decided he liked being her best. "I'd say the same to you."

She snuggled into his shoulder and brought up the picture of Pete again. "I'll call the shelter tomorrow. I'll get all the stuff he'll need. Don't worry. I'll take care of everything."

"I don't mind helping." He turned a page in his magazine. "I like cats. Mostly mellow, but sometimes a bit mad. They suit me."

"Oh! Gavin, the show's back."

He turned his attention back to the dancers. She'd closed her tablet when the announcer said the final couple's name.

"They're doing the tango for their final! I've been waiting weeks to see this." She was practically bouncing on the couch.

It was so damn adorable, he wanted to take a picture.

Fuck me. I'm going to end up taking tango lessons, aren't I?

Chloe's eyes were raptly watching every moment of the sensual dance on screen. Her mouth was open a little, and her fingers tapped out the beat on her thigh.

Yes, you are, Wallace. And you're going to like it.

THE END

AFTERWORD

February 26, 2019

Dear Readers,

Thanks for returning to the Elemental Legacy series. I hope you enjoyed reading *The Devil and the Dancer* as much as I enjoyed writing it. (Which was a lot!)

Very soon into the drafting of *Blood Apprentice*, I knew that Gavin and Chloe—who had been such an amazing part of *Midnight Labyrinth*—would not be in the second Elemental Legacy novel much. Their story had gone in a different direction than Ben and Tenzin's. I knew they needed their own book.

And I loved writing it! Gavin and Chloe are such vibrant characters. I hope you know this isn't the end of their story. They'll be showing up in future Elemental Legacy novels and they could easily get another novella. But for right now, I like to think of them hanging out in their apartment, kissing a lot, dancing, dreaming, and getting to know Pete.

Currently, I'm working in my contemporary romance series, *Love Stories on 7th and Main,* for a couple books. I'm drafting Tayla's story, HOOKED, right now, and I included a preview at the end of this book.

After my 7th & Main work, I'll be back with Ben and Tenzin for the third and fourth Elemental Legacy novels, which have not been titled yet.

I hope you take the time to sign up for my newsletter or my blog at ElizabethHunterWrites.com to keep up with all the latest news, teasers, and contests happening for my books.

And of course, honest reviews at your favorite retailer are always very welcome and help a writer out!

Thanks for reading,

Elizabeth Hunter

PREVIEW: HOOKED

Tayla McKinnon took one step outside, glanced at the profusion of blossoms on the pear trees lining Main Street in Metlin, California, and reached for her handkerchief. She brought the delicately embroidered cotton square to her face.

3…2…1…

"ACHOO!" She let out a massive sneeze that made her eyes water. Luckily, it would *not* smudge her makeup.

Waterproof mascara, T. Waterproof mascara is your friend.

"Hey Tayla!" Ethan Vasquez stepped outside his hardware store and set up an angled chalkboard on the sidewalk, highlighting the classes he was offering that week. "How ya doing this morning?"

Tayla strolled toward him, keeping her handkerchief in her hand. "How much longer do these trees bloom?"

Ethan glanced up at the masses of white blooms. "The pear trees?"

Tayla blinked away the tears in her eyes. "No, the other trees making me sneeze."

He gave her a crooked grin. "Well, there are the almonds, the olives, the apricots, the—"

"Ahhhh!" She threw her head back. "Why did I move to farm country?"

"I'm just saying, it could be any of those." He shrugged. "But it's probably the pears. My mom's allergic too."

Tayla wasn't from Metlin. She was from San Francisco. A native of the cosmopolitan and cultured City on the Bay. The city that *didn't* have pear trees everywhere. How the hell did she end up sneezing in Metlin?

"Tay!" A voice came from behind her.

Tayla turned and saw her best friend and roommate, Emmie Elliot, poking her head out of the bookshop and tattoo studio she ran with her boyfriend, Ox. Emmie sold books; Ox was a tattoo artist. Their shop, INK, had been a gamble that turned into a slowly growing success.

It was also the reason Tayla was in Metlin. She'd moved the year before the help Emmie fulfill her dream. She worked part time in the shop and lived rent-free in the second floor apartment with Emmie. Tayla had also started her own bookkeeping business that was taking off with the merchants in downtown Metlin. It was light years away from the corporate accounting job she'd held in San Francisco.

"Hey." Emmie walked out of the store with bare feet. She looked like she'd just stumbled out of bed and her hair was twisted into a messy knot on her head.

Tayla surveyed the fashion disaster that was her best friend. "Did you just wake up?"

"Kinda?"

Tayla shook her head in wonder. She'd been up for over two hours. She'd curled and fixed her hair, done her makeup, and chosen the perfect outfit to compliment her voluptuous figure. She was a fashion blogger in addition to being a bookkeeper. Her hustle was strong, and she did *not* walk out the door without her face and outfit perfect.

"Why did I come out here?" Emmie looked half asleep and definitely caffeine deprived. "Oh! Right. Did you want to meet at Daisy's for lunch?"

Tayla mentally scrolled through her calendar. "I have meetings at ten and eleven, but I'm supposed to do Daisy's books around two, so yes. I'll meet you there at... twelve-thirty?"

"Ox should be able to watch the shop." Emmie walked toward her and pulled a small pack of tissues from her pocket. "Also, the handkerchief is cute, but this is spring in Metlin. You need the heavy duty stuff."

"Fine." Tayla reluctantly took the small tissue package with the words "now with more aloe!" on the side. "I bow to your rural living experience."

"And this." Emmie handed over a bubbled strip of pills. "Antihistamines. Every day, Tayla. You have to take them every day."

Tayla took the pills. "Why do you want to live here again?"

"Because it's beautiful, close to the mountains, has great farmers' markets, and I'll be able to afford to buy a house before I'm fifty."

She rolled her eyes. "Fine."

"I love you."

"Love you too." Tayla dropped the pills and the tissues into her bright pink shoulder bag. "But I don't love your trees." She put on her sunglasses and started walking toward the lot where she parked her car, then she turned and glanced back at the shop.

Light. Pretty white blossoms on scattered on the sidewalk. Empty sidewalks.

"Stop!" She held up her hand. "Emmie, before you go back inside—"

"Morning outfit pic?"

"Yes." Tayla took the bag off her shoulder and adjusted the belt on the yellow and pink striped wrap-dress to adjust the amount of cleavage it showed. "They just sent me this bag and the light is perfect for spring photos with the flowers and everything."

She hurried back to Emmie and the line of blooming pear trees. "Can you prop the shop door open?" She glanced at the adorable new yellow bike Emmie had bought the month before that was chained to the rack in front of the shop. "That's good if we can get it in the background. I think if I stand here..." She looked up. "Ethan, can you shake this tree a little bit?"

Ethan, who'd been leaning in his doorway looking bemused at the impromptu photo shoot, frowned. "You're already sneezing and you want me to shake *more* pollen on you?"

Noooooo, her nose yelled. She glanced at the bright vegan "leather" bag she'd been given and thought about handbag hashtags, follower counts, and her bank account. "Yeah. More flowers."

Emmie took Tayla's phone and opened the camera

while Tayla positioned herself under the pear tree, gave her makeup a quick check—gold framed sunglasses on *point*—and held the bag in both hands, pushing her bust together as she positioned herself under the tree, looked up, and let out a fake laugh.

"It's so weird when you do that," Ethan said, reaching up with a rake and shaking one of the pear tree branches. White flower petals rained down on the sidewalk and onto Tayla.

"Fake laugh equals real smile," Tayla said. She changed positions a few times. Put the bag over her shoulder. Looked at the camera. Then away from it. Turned and walked away. Turned back. "Emmie, how we doing?" She could feel her nose starting to twitch.

"Give me one more..." Emmie stepped back, then stepped forward. "The light is tricky..." She took a few more pictures and held out the phone. "Check em."

Tayla held her handkerchief to her nose and scrolled quickly through the photos. "I can use at least three of these and the bag looks amazing." She slipped the phone in the bag just as the sneeze worked its way out.

"ACHOO!" She gave up on her embroidered handkerchief and blew her nose with the paper tissues. "These *trees*." She leaned over and kissed Emmie's cheek quickly. "You're the best. Thank you."

"It's kind of chilly." Emmie looked down at her feet. "Have I been barefoot this whole time?"

"Yes. Go back inside before Ox comes and yells at me for making your precious little feet cold." She turned Emmie by the shoulders and shoved her toward the door.

"See you at lunch. Don't forget to post on the blog today. With pictures! Don't forget the pictures."

"Okay." Emmie waved over her shoulder. "See you."

Ethan walked back to his shop and propped the rake against the front of his display windows. "What about me? Do I get a kiss, too?"

Tayla sashayed over to his doorway and crooked her finger at him. "Better believe it, handsome."

Tayla kissed Ethan's bearded cheek when he leaned down. Then she pulled away just as another sneeze exploded from her nose. "I think I'm allergic to you, too."

"Nah." He grinned. "But I bet Jeremy would like it if you were."

"Hush." She shooed him away with a smile and a flip of her manicured hand. "Don't start trouble."

Ethan was an adorable bear of a man. Tall, broad shoulders, and a belly that said he enjoyed a pint at the ice house after work. He loved live music, dancing, and binging the latest sci-fi or fantasy series on the weekend. He drove a big pick-up truck and liked his women with more than a handful of ass.

In short, he was exactly Tayla's type.

And yet... no chemistry. None.

"Bye!" She walked down Main Street and turned right at the crosswalk. On the corner of Main and Ash was the dark windows of No Cape Comics where the man who was definitely *not* Tayla's type would be opening his door in about an hour.

Jeremy Allen was sweet, geeky, clever, and handsome as sin. In addition to loving comics and games, he loved everything about the outdoors. He climbed mountains in his spare time. He camped. He fished. He rode down mountains on his bike.

Tayla was a yoga enthusiast and *loved* to dance. She had a bike, but she wasn't crazy enough to take it down mountains. Hiking and fishing? Not her scene. So much dirt. So many bugs. She liked nature... through the pristine window of a well-furnished hotel.

Jeremy was also loyal, family-oriented, and had "long term romantic partner" written all over his gorgeous face.

Tayla wasn't interested in long term anything. She liked variety. In fashion, in work, and in men. Who could handle one person for the rest of your life? She'd be bored to tears.

And yet...

Even walking by his shop gave her goosebumps.

So. Inconvenient.

Tayla glanced at Jeremy's store and kept walking. She had a lot to do that day. The last thing she should be thinking about was a man who shouldn't move past the flirting stage.

Tayla McKinnon had a life and a plan. Jeremy Allen wasn't part of it.

Find out more about the 7th & Main series at ElizabethHunterWrites.com.
And grab the first book, INK, right now in e-book, audiobook, or paperback at your favorite retailer!

ACKNOWLEDGMENTS

To my family, American and Ethiopian, who supported me during the holidays when I was writing this book, thank you. It was a hard season for me, and all of you gave me the strength, prayers, space, and encouragement to finish. I love you all so very much.

To all my readers who begged me for more Gavin and Chloe, I want to send a sincere thanks. I hope you enjoyed *The Devil and the Dancer*. I absolutely loved writing it, and I'm sure I'll end up writing more.

A special thanks goes to Danielle Aretz, who lent me her dancing expertise for this story. I am not a dancer, I just write one on the internets. Any mistakes are unintentional and wholly my own.

To Cat Bowen, my Scottish Profanity Beta. Your talents

are multitude. Your slang incomprehensible. I could not write Gavin without you.

To all my whiskey drinkers out there, cheers! Hope you enjoyed a nice glass of your favorite whiskey with Gavin. Upon release, I will be enjoying a glass of Oban in his honor.

To my Jenn and my Gen. You're the two best assistants ever. I cannot make life happen without you.

Thanks to my amazing editing team, Amy Cissell, and Anne and Linda at Victory Editing.

Thanks to Alisha and all the folks at Damonza for this AMAZINGLY GORGEOUS book cover! I love it. So much. So very much.

Thanks to my PR team at Social Butterfly PR. Emily, you are *the best*!

And to Abay and all the staff at Bethel Hotel in Ziway, thanks for delivering food and drinks to the crazy American writer in residence. Thanks for being our home away from home in Ethiopia.

ABOUT THE AUTHOR

ELIZABETH HUNTER is a *USA Today* and international best-selling author of romance, contemporary fantasy, and paranormal mystery. Based in Central California, she travels extensively to write fantasy fiction exploring world mythologies, history, and the universal bonds of love, friendship, and family. She has published over thirty works of fiction and sold over a million books worldwide. She is the author of Love Stories on 7th and Main, the Elemental Legacy series, the Irin Chronicles, the Cambio Springs Mysteries, and other works of fiction.

ALSO BY ELIZABETH HUNTER

The Elemental Legacy

Shadows and Gold

Imitation and Alchemy

Omens and Artifacts

Midnight Labyrinth

Blood Apprentice

The Devil and the Dancer

The Elemental Mysteries

A Hidden Fire

This Same Earth

The Force of Wind

A Fall of Water

The Stars Afire

The Elemental World

Building From Ashes

Waterlocked

Blood and Sand

The Bronze Blade

The Scarlet Deep

A Very Proper Monster

A Stone-Kissed Sea

The Irin Chronicles

The Scribe

The Singer

The Secret

The Staff and the Blade

The Silent

The Storm

The Seeker

The Cambio Springs Series

Long Ride Home

Shifting Dreams

Five Mornings

Desert Bound

Waking Hearts

Contemporary Romance

The Genius and the Muse

7th and Main

INK

HOOKED (Spring 2019)

Linx & Bogie Mysteries

A Ghost in the Glamour

A Bogie in the Boat

Made in the USA
Columbia, SC
06 August 2022

64756642R00098